FAE FORGED AXES & CHIN WAXES

MYSTICAL MIDLIFE IN MAINE BOOK 8

BRENDA TRIM

Learn from yesterday, live for today, hope for tomorrow.

CHAPTER 1

"Mom! I think someone murdered dad!" My body jackknifed to a sitting position the instant I heard Nina's words.

Aidoneus was out of bed a second later. "Does she mean your father? I thought he died a long time ago."

My heart hammered in my chest as I got up and slipped my feet into my slippers before grabbing my robe. "No, she means her father. Shit, shit, shit. I bet it was those damn vampires thinking they were hurting me by killing the asshole."

Aidoneus had his jeans on and was in the process of pulling a shirt over his head. He looked at me with misery in his expression. "We will find out who did this and make them pay."

He was the best partner a woman could ask for. It was clear getting revenge for the death of my ex-husband hurt him in ways I could understand, but that didn't stop him from being at my side, promising to help make the culprit pay.

I shook my head. "First of all, we don't know that's what happened. And if someone did kill Miles, I'd be tempted to give them a gift basket."

He chuckled and wrapped an arm around my waist. "I'm coming!" I shouted to Nina, making my mom and Nana come out of their bedrooms.

Nana smoothed her wayward silver curls. "Why is she shouting across the house instead of coming to get you?"

I shrugged my shoulders and looked down at my daughter, who was running down the hall when we got to the door. "What happened?"

Nina thrust my phone into my hand when I reached her. "You got a call from an unknown number. The guy said there was a dead body you needed to investigate." Her voice was high-pitched and full of panic.

One of my eyebrows rose to my hairline as my mouth compressed into a thin line. Nana spoke before I managed a response. "Child, you never make a huge fuss over an anonymous call about a dead body. You have no way of knowing that was your father. Sweet, Jesus. Raising the alarm like that and scaring an old woman like me out of a deep sleep could have given me a heart attack."

Nina's cheeks turned pink as I walked past her with Aidon at my side. "But, Nana, you don't understand. The guy said the body was found in the same park where dad goes running every morning. What are the chances someone calls you about a dead guy in North Carolina in the *same* location I know dad was an hour ago?"

I stopped at the bottom of the grand staircase and looked back up at my daughter. There were fine lines around her mouth and eyes which had the shine of unshed tears in them. I reached for her hand and squeezed. "We will get to the bottom of it. Let's get some coffee, so my brain is fully functional, and we can go from there."

I walked into the kitchen to find Mythia flitting around. Flour covered her dark burgundy goth clothes and the island. It looked like she was making crepes. "I figured you could use some breakfast now that you're all up. Do you think it's true? That someone killed your ex-husband?"

There was more to the pixie's worry than her concern for Nina, or even me. If I had to guess, she was worried about people being killed that were connected to me. It was a significant concern. I had enemies coming at me from every direction. Most of whom I didn't even know existed. It was the price of my position in the magical world.

"I have no idea, Thia, but I'm going to figure it out." I opened my phone and pulled up a phone number I never thought I would use again. My hand shook as I held it to my ear.

Aidoneus handed me a cup of coffee and stood pressed against my back. I took a sip while the phone rang. The hot liquid got stuck in my throat and I had to force it past the knot.

"Are the kids alright?" I exhaled the breath I was holding when my ex-husband answered my call.

A smile spread over my face as relief made me slightly dizzy. I was not looking forward to having to explain his demise to my kids. Not to mention people would think me cold when I didn't mourn his loss.

"The kids are fine. Nina was worried about you and, uh, I told her I would make sure you were alright," I explained, not having thought up another excuse for my call.

"I know you're not calling for our daughter, but I'm not surprised you miss me," Miles replied.

There was a split second when I was back in our marriage, and he was telling me not to wear leggings because my cellulite was visible. Suddenly, I was a millimeter tall and an incompetent wife that didn't know how to dress herself or take care of the kids properly.

Forget that shit. You are a freaking rockstar, Pheebs!

I shoved aside the doubt those thoughts brought on and snorted into the phone. "You no longer own real estate in my mind. Not when I have Aidon who is your better in every way. Here's your daughter."

I thrust my phone at Nina, so she could talk to her lunatic of a father. I would never keep my kids from speaking to him, or from seeing him when they wanted, but I was not subjecting myself to any more of his abuse. I did my duty as a parent and made the call. I would always protect Nina and Jean-Marc from as much of the shit in life as possible.

Focusing on the good in my life, I turned to Aidon. "Would you text Stella and ask her to come over since Nina is on my phone? I want to know why someone is calling about a dead body in North Carolina."

He grabbed his phone from the charger on the desk built into one corner of the kitchen. "I don't like that this body was located so close to a park that Miles frequents. This could be a message to you."

I inclined my head as I watched Nina to make sure she didn't hear his comment. "That's what I'm afraid of. I'm tempted to ignore it and let the jackass be injured. His ego is bigger than your father's, which is saying something."

Nana pursed her lips like she'd just sucked on a lemon. "Now, you're just insulting Hades. Miles is an idiot that doesn't know his head from his asshole and should never be in the same sentence as a powerful god. Even if said god thinks he's the center of the universe."

I chuckled and took a seat on one of the stools. "Fair point, Nana. There is a chance this is just another case for me to handle. Do we know where the closest paranormal police officer is located right now? If I'm getting called about this, the victim is likely one of us, so we can't allow the mundane authorities to get ahold of the body."

Selene and Layla walked into the kitchen from the back-yard. Both were covered in sweat from the training they'd been doing early each morning. Layla's expression went from relaxed to alert in an instant. "What happened?"

I explained about the call and our theories as to why I was called. Layla blew out a breath when I finished and shook her head. "Aidon's right. Your ex might be a target, and this was a warning shot."

Nina's gasp made me cringe. She'd hung up the phone in time to hear Layla's comment. There was no way I was going to sugarcoat it or give her false reassurances. The last thing she needed was for me to tell her something I couldn't guarantee.

"*Set aside the personal element to this case. Treat it like you would anything else. And start your investigation by trying to trace the phone call.*" I looked around, searching for my familiar. She was perched next to my mom on a stool. I hadn't seen her join us.

Selene jumped up and grabbed her laptop from the desk. It turned out she was a whiz with the thing. She could find just about anything on the internet, as well as create apps to help keep me organized. Running a multi-billion-dollar corporation while trying to juggle cases involving demons, evil witches, and other supernatural creatures was too much for a simple calendar.

"I can hack into the cell towers and locate the caller," Selene said as her fingers flew over the keyboard.

Layla leaned over her shoulder. "Once you find him, can we continue to follow his movements? It'll take us time to make arrangements and get to North Carolina."

Selene was entirely focused on what she was doing, so I didn't think she was going to respond. "Once I get his number, I can find him anywhere in the world. That's the beauty of technology."

Aidoneus shook his head as he put a crepe on a plate and added fresh strawberries. My stomach rumbled at the sight of the delicious food. "That's terrifying. Magic isn't as effective at following people. The longer I'm here, the more I understand why paranormals are afraid of being discovered. Mundies are capable of some truly terrifying things."

The ringing of the doorbell interrupted our conversation. Stella must have already been on her way. I was about to answer it when Aidon put the plate in front of me, then kissed my lips and loped off barefoot to answer my door. My heart melted with the love and affection he showed me daily. It wasn't something I'd had before, but I would never settle for less. Of course, I didn't see myself ever leaving Aidon.

I groaned after shoving a bite of the crepe and fruit into my mouth. "This is the best I've ever eaten, Thia. Between you and my mom, I'm going to weigh a ton by the time the holidays roll around."

"You're too busy running from Tainted witches and demons to gain that much weight," Stella teased as she and Aidoneus joined us in the kitchen. "You need all this delicious food to keep your sexy curves."

I smiled at my best friend, grateful we had reconnected when I moved back home. Stella and I had been BFFs since kindergarten. We'd drifted apart after college, when I had married Miles. Years later, Facebook brought us back into each other's lives, but it wasn't the same as living close to one another. I couldn't have picked a better partner to go through my magical makeover with. Stella was optimistic, sunny, upbeat, and always put together. I was apprehensive, sarcastic, and more often than not, saw the negative side of things.

"I'm in no danger of losing these hips." I patted the cushion of flesh on my sides.

Aidoneus grabbed me around the waist. "I love your body. You are perfect in every way. You could gain or lose weight, and you would still be the sexiest woman alive."

Nina scrunched up her face and stuck her fingers in her ears. "Nah, nah, nah, nah. I'm not hearing this."

"You need to hear this, daughter. You should never settle for someone that doesn't completely adore you. Life is too short for anything less." I gave Nina a smile, then lifted my face to Aidon for a kiss.

Breaking away before our lip lock got me too heated, I focused on my crepe while sharing the details of the morning with Stella. She fixed herself a crepe and stood near me, at the end of the island.

Nana bit into the crepe and widened her eyes. Her gaze shifted to my mom. "Is this whipped cream made with one of your experimental recipes?"

I cocked my head, watching my mother's cheeks turn pink. "Yeah. I infused the cream with a potion designed to enhance flavors. I've also got chocolate chip cookies that have an energy boost bigger than if you had a quad shot espresso."

Mythia waved the tool that looked like a knife used to spread frosting on cakes at my mom. "Don't forget about your cheerful cherry pie or blissed out blueberry pancakes."

My mom's eyes lit up. "I came up with another last night. Chill out cheesecake."

My jaw dropped while Nina squeaked. "Were those cookies in the pantry yesterday, Gammy?"

"Yes, I made them the night before and put them in the Tupperware bin before going to bed," my mom replied.

Nina covered her face with her hands. "Oh no. I gave a baggie of those to my English teacher trying to get on her good side. No wonder she was practically running around the school at lunchtime. What do I do?"

Nana threw her head back and laughed. "You do nothing. It is temporary and won't hurt her. Your Gammy would never make something that would harm anyone else. Besides, that tight-assed woman needed them. Although the chill out cheesecake would be a better choice next time."

"Nana is right. The cookies likely wore off by the time she got home and won't hurt her," my mom added.

Selene paused in her typing and lifted her head. "I might need some of those if this guy remains as elusive as it seems right now. The park Nina told me about had very few pings that early in the morning. Whoever it was seems to be hiding from us."

Stella cocked her head as she popped a blueberry into her mouth. "Do you think we could scry for this person?"

I shrugged my shoulders. "It might be worth a try. But first, I need to find out if my company has any connections in the coroner's office. I want to make sure the body doesn't fall into mundie hands."

Aidoneus swallowed the massive bite he'd shoved into his mouth. "Let me work on that. I can have one of my agents intercept the mundane authorities if the body has been found."

"Thank you, Yahweh." I ran a hand down his chest before he walked out of the room to make his calls.

Layla lifted her fork. "Tseki has some friends in that area. I'll go wake him up and ask him to give them a call. They live there and should be able to get to the scene right away."

"Won't it be suspicious if a bunch of odd-looking people try to take the body from police? We will need a vampire to erase any memory of a murder in a park." Stella visibly shuddered as she spoke of the creatures that almost killed her during our trip to New Orleans.

I squeezed her hand. "I'm hoping no one has found the person yet. Go ask Tseki to call his friends while we try to scry for the caller."

Layla nodded and took off out the back door. She had become a close friend since she tried to save me from Myrna all those months ago. She was also invaluable in helping me adjust to this new life. I could always count on her and Tsekani. They had been Hattie's bodyguards and were now mine. Although they both did so much more for me.

My mom chewed on her lower lip. "Are you sure you should look for him? It's more than likely he killed this person. Otherwise, how did he know to call us?"

Nina set her plate in the sink, then turned to look at me. "It's probably a moot point, Gammy. We don't have anything of the caller's to use for scrying."

Stella picked up my cell phone and pressed on the phone app. "What if we use this incoming call? It's the closest thing to his person that we have."

My mother set a pan on the island. "I'll grab the herbs from the workroom downstairs. What do we need again? Fennel, basil, clove, hibiscus, meadow-sweet, orange and lavender?"

"Yep. I'll get the pot on to boil." I filled the pot with water from the tap, but Stella stopped me when I went to put it on the stove.

"Let's use magic to heat it," she suggested.

I smiled back at her. "I'll hold the pot while you use your fire." Stella was a natural with magic. Everything came easy to her, where I had to study and practice for days before I was able to do the simplest thing. Having her use her fire was safer than letting my mom or Nana and allowed me to stir the mixture while it boiled.

Nina was carrying the black candles when she and my mom came back into the room. My mom added the herbs while Nina set the candles around the bowl on the island. Nana rooted around in the big green purse I'd bought her online to replace the cursed one we had to destroy. It was a designer bag but didn't compare to the Gucci she'd bought at the antique store. "Aha! I'm going to add our question in writing, as well. I read in our family grimoire that burning it over the water will add to the power of the scry."

Stella tapped her lip. "Do we need the jasmine incense?"

Nina held up a brown cone. "I've got it."

"I have two agents heading to the park now. They're an hour away," Aidoneus said as he came back in to the kitchen.

Layla entered the backdoor at the same time. "Tseki is calling his friends who are in town. He'll be here in a bit. What are we doing?"

"Scrying for the caller and possible murderer," I explained as I poured the heated scrying water into the bowl.

Nana grabbed a lighter, held the paper over the bowl, then lit it. She dropped it right away and Mythia flew forward and used her control over the air element to keep the burning paper floating.

I held the desire to know the location of the caller in my mind and shoved all other thoughts aside. "Mihi quid quaero."

The water turned opaque as my magic built around us. The air crackled with power and lightning flashed across the surface of the water for several seconds until it cleared to show me my favorite coffee shop not far from my old house.

Nina gasped. "He's still there. We need to leave."

I held up my hand. "I'm not entirely certain how we are going to handle this, but we aren't going in without a thorough plan. We can't chance this being a trap. I've built enough of a reputation for going the extra mile on cases that an enemy could use a report of a dead body as a way to get me in his clutches."

Aidoneus inclined his head as he looked at me. I could see the pride shining there. I'd learned a lot from him. In fact, more and more I heard his voice in my head when I faced different situations. It was nice to have someone believe in me and give me the knowledge I needed to succeed without him. That was a sign of true love, in my opinion.

CHAPTER 2

"*J*aylin is searching the park right now." Tseki paced the kitchen back and forth.

Ever since his previous boyfriend, Brody, betrayed him and convinced a pissed-off witch to curse me, Tseki had kept his distance. Something happened recently when Tseki'd taken a vacation. He was less withdrawn and smiled more often. I thought he had met someone new, but doubted I would get to meet the guy any time soon. I made a mental note to talk to him about it later. He didn't need to keep his private life separate from us. Not that he had to share it with us, either. I wanted him to feel free to let us know he could talk to us.

"Does he have someone with him? I'm worried this is a trap meant for me." I didn't want anyone falling into it because of me.

Tseki stopped pacing and accepted the mug of coffee my mom handed him. "Thank you. Jay took his alpha and several pack members with him. He also called Mohan and told him about the call, so we can keep the paranormal police up to date."

Layla twisted her lips to the side. "And what did Mohan say? Leave it to the Pleiades?"

Tseki snorted, then coughed as he choked on the liquid he was in the process of swallowing. "Did you expect anything less?"

Layla shook her head. Nina sat next to Nana, watching the discussion. She was chewing on her thumbnail. I knew she was worried about her father, and I couldn't fault her for that. But I couldn't reassure her. It sucked not to be able to tell her that everything was going to be okay. In the magical world, I'd learned enough to know nothing was guaranteed.

"We need to make travel arrangements. I'll text Morgan and have her make some calls." I'd promoted the witch after her daughter cursed me with Brody's help. Morgan had become an invaluable resource in my business, as well as becoming an assistant of sorts, sharing the task with Lilith.

Nana pursed her lips. "Why do you have to go? Make this Mohan deal with it. You have enough on your plate here."

I cocked my head to the side. "Someone called me. That tells me that this death is bigger than we know. Or they are baiting me. Either way, I need to be the one to deal with it." I sent Morgan the message telling her what I needed.

Aidoneus stood up from where he'd been leaning against the counter. "I want to agree with Amelia, but I see your point. If you ignore this, and it's an attempt to get at you, someone else could be killed and I know you well enough that you will blame yourself. I'll go pack while you make the rest of the arrangements."

I lifted my head for a kiss before he left through the back-door. Nina stood up and moved toward the stairs. "I'll pack, as well."

I shook my head. "Oh no you don't missy. You'll be staying here."

Tseki's phone rang, cutting off Nina's angry retort. Tseki pressed the screen. "Hey, Jay. What did you find?"

The sound of feet shuffling echoed through the speaker, followed by the inhale of a breath. "You were right, Tseki. There's a dead elf here. She was placed behind some shrubs to keep her hidden from mundies. The woman suffered a violent death. There are several large cuts covering her body. But that's not all. There's something off about the way she feels. I can't put my finger on it. Neither can my alpha. Is your Pleiades coming down? Or should we contact the closest elves to deal with the dead woman?"

I suddenly understood why people like Myrna thought she could get away with bullying Hattie into giving them her magic. There was no communication between species. And there was very little oversight. I would have thought that the severe punishments doled out for breaking the few rules that existed would make most think twice. But, if there's no one to enforce the consequences, no one would expect to be caught.

I dipped my head at Tseki. He inclined his head, then focused on the phone. "I have Phoebe here with me. We are making arrangements now."

"Hi, Jay. This is Phoebe. Can you tell me if there are any magical traps in the area? My family is concerned this is a trap meant for me," I added before Tseki could hang up the phone.

"Nice to speak with you, Pleiades. I understand your family's concern. I don't believe there is anything to be worried about. We searched the park with care, paying close attention to any magic we came across. We made it through most of the park before finding the victim and didn't encounter anything out of the ordinary. Like I told Tseki, there is a magical signature surrounding the body, but we can't identify it. We can have a local witch look at the elf if you'd like." Jay's respect was something I had come to expect from most shifters. They were taught it from birth, through the hierarchy of their packs.

"That won't be necessary." I don't know these witches and don't want to involve them unless necessary. "Is your alpha there? I'd like to ask the pack to keep the body safe until I get there. I have someone looking for a house for us to rent while we investigate." Given the nature of the case, a hotel would not suit our needs. They may not be too impressed if we were to walk in carrying a dead body.

There was a rustling sound that echoed through the speaker before another voice responded to me. "Pleiades, this is Kason Sanders, alpha of Jaylin's pack. We would be happy to keep the body safe as long as the paranormal police agree. The pack will not be getting on the bad side of the officers. Our young have enough trouble controlling their urges. We don't need to be scrutinized any closer."

I wasn't sure what to think of that. I didn't like the idea of shifters acting out then flying under the radar. *You can't police the entire magical world, nor should you.* Shaking off those thoughts, I refocused on the matter at hand. "I believe Tsekani contacted Mohan, and he said to leave it to me."

Kason's scoff sounded through the phone. "That was before there was a body. He needs to be notified. I'll remove the body before mundies start flocking to the area. Let him know that when you speak with him."

I lifted a brow as I looked at Tseki, then Layla. Both shrugged their shoulders. I sighed, suddenly not looking forward to talking to Mohan. "I will let him know. Can you gather any items that contain magical energy close to the victim? It will help give me a complete picture of what happened to her. Pictures would also be nice to have."

"Jay has already photographed the area. We will gather what we can. Do you know who called to inform you about the dead elf? I can speak with them and get more information for you." From what Tseki shared with me, Kason didn't seem like the kind of alpha that did anything out of the kindness of his heart. No doubt he wanted to see if the caller was the killer.

I briefly debated what to tell him. It wouldn't be the worst thing if he was able to locate and detain the guy that called me. "All we know is that less than half an hour ago, he was at the Beanery coffee shop a few miles from the park. It's not much to go on, but we know nothing outside of that."

"I'll send a team to check the place out. If we find anything, I'll let you know," Kason promised.

I thanked him, then hung up the phone. I set my empty coffee mug in the sink and leaned on the island. "I know many of you want to go with me on this one. Nina, I need you to stay here. You can't miss school and I don't want you in danger. I know it doesn't seem fair, but you're my baby and I won't be able to concentrate if I know you are there in the middle of the fight."

Nina scowled and crossed her arms over her chest. Nana bumped Nina's shoulder. "We will practice spells and potions while she's gone, so when it's time for you to join her, you'll be ready."

My mom nodded in agreement. "That's the best way to get your mom to agree to take you one day."

"I'll help train you. I bet Layla will too if she stays," Selene offered.

I couldn't be more grateful for the family I'd surrounded myself with. They looked out for my daughter, mom, and Nana when I couldn't. It's the only reason I was ever able to leave Camden. "I'm not going to like it, no matter what. However, I won't keep you away forever. I can agree that knowing you can fight back will make it easier on my nerves when your time comes."

Nina stood up and wrapped an arm around my shoulders. "That's fair enough, mom. It's harder to stay this time knowing you're going to be close to dad and Jean-Marc."

I smiled and tucked a strand of hair behind her ear. "I don't plan on seeing your father, but I will give your brother your love."

Tsekani tapped the dark screen of his cell phone. "You should call Mohan and let him know the update."

My stomach turned over at the same time sweat beaded on my spine. "I can't put it off forever, can I?"

Tseki laughed. "No, you can't." He opened the phone and pressed the phone app. After hitting a contact, he thrust the phone at me.

My hands shook as I grabbed it, and I almost dropped the device. After the third ring, I was convinced no one was answering, so I jumped when the deep voice barked, "What?" into the phone.

I bristled at his tone, as if he was being bothered by being called. "Is this Mohan? This is the Pleiades, Phoebe Dieudonne`." I rarely used my title, but this guy's attitude didn't sit well with me.

"Yes, I'm Mohan. Are you calling to tell me to deal with the report on my own?" The paranormal police officer bristled with every word.

I scoffed, embracing the fact that I was more capable of handling investigations than this guy. "Actually no, I'm not. The pack alpha, Kason, asked that I call and inform you he is taking the victim from the scene, and keeping her for me, until I can get down to North Carolina. The *only* reason I'm calling at all is a courtesy to him."

The sound of Mahon growling almost made me laugh. "You are not an officer of magical law. If there was a death, I will handle it."

"How many officers are there in the United States?"

"There is one officer per region, Northern part, Eastern section, Western and Southern. NC straddles southern and eastern and I split the state with Terrance," Mahon explained.

I couldn't believe how few officers they have to cover such large areas. It wasn't possible for them to do an adequate job. I understood, even more, how and why people started coming to Hattie. I doubted she would be able to ignore these cases any more than I could.

"I was called about this case. I will be handling it. You stay where you're at and deal with the many other cases that I'm sure are on your plate. Not only am I far more capable of solving this crime, I'm the most powerful magical being in the United States. There isn't anyone better suited than me." I cringed when the words came out of my mouth. I didn't boast about my power or abilities, but I needed to send him a clear message.

"Bu...no...you can't take this case. An officer should investigate the death," Mahon insisted.

"You were all too happy to leave me to look into the call. Now that you know there's a body, you insist it be you? I'm not going to tell you this again. You've already given me the case. I am handling it and if you get in my way, you will regret it."

Nana chuckled. "You tell him, Phoebe." I smirked at her.

Mohan cleared his throat. "I fear we got off on the wrong foot. I concede the case is yours. Please let me know if you need any help."

"You'll be my first call. I'll keep you posted. There is no way to tell yet what motivated this murder, but the shifters made it clear the woman's demise was violent. How much domestic violence do you see in the magical world? In the mundie world, the first suspect is always the husband or boyfriend." I imagined it was the same, but wanted confirmation.

"We have our fair share of domestic disputes. However, if the woman has mated, you can rule him out. Most that choose to bond with another because they found their true mate would die without them. Making the spouse a second victim of the murder," Mohan explained.

"I'll be in touch when I have more information." I hung up and thought about what I needed to do before I left for North Carolina.

My to-do list popped into my mind, immediately overwhelming me. One item stuck out as I mentally wiped the board clear. "I have something I want to do before we leave." A smile spread over my face when I saw Aidon crossing my backyard through the forest that led to his.

Stella wagged her finger at me. "I'm all for getting stuff done, but doing your boyfriend doesn't count as an adequate reason to postpone a murder investigation."

My jaw dropped to my chest at the same time Aidoneus walked through the door. "What did I miss?"

Stella and Layla started laughing while I rolled my eyes at them. "Ignore the childish duo over there. I was just about to tell them what I want to do before we leave."

Aidon looked from my friends to me. "The grin on their faces tells me they had naked shenanigans in mind. I can tell from your response I'm not getting that lucky, so what is it you'd like to do?"

I lifted one corner of my mouth and shook my head. "I'm going to pay Marius a visit, and I'd like you and Stella to accompany me, while Layla and Tsekani are close by as backup."

Stella's smile disappeared at the same time her face turned white as a sheet. "Uh, I'm not so sure about that."

I gasped and grabbed her hands in mine. "Ah shit. I'm sorry, Stella. I wasn't thinking. You go home and pack if you'd like to come to North Carolina with us while the four of us deliver my message to the nasty vampire."

One of Aidoneus's eyebrows lifted to his hairline. "Why do you want to do this now? I assume you want to go tonight so we can leave tomorrow. That doesn't leave us much time to prepare adequately for either event."

Letting go of Stella's hands, I crossed to the fridge and grabbed an energy drink. The coffee wasn't enough for what I had to do today. "If I wait until we get back, I will lose all effectiveness in sending the entire vampire population a message not to mess with me and my loved ones. I've already waited longer than I'd like. We have no idea how long this case will take, and I'm not willing to put anyone left behind in danger. If he thinks he's frightened me, there's no saying what he will do next."

Aidoneus's gaze held mine for several seconds. "I can deliver the message for you. There's no need for you to go anywhere near him."

It was my turn to glare at the love of my life. Sometimes, I adored how protective he was. And at others, I bristled against what felt like control. I took a deep breath to calm my anger. "You know that isn't going to work with Marius. He had the balls to send vampires after us in New Orleans. They attacked when Stella and I were most vulnerable and nearly killed her. They did kill a couple of innocent mundies. That's a death sentence right there. Are you saying they will be frightened of me if you send the message for me? In fact, I think you need to stay outside with Layla and Tseki because I cannot have you fighting my battles for me, nor can I appear to be leaning on you for support."

Stella chewed on her bottom lip. "As much as I hate the idea of you going in there without me or Aidon, I see the reason it's necessary. If you face them alone, it tells the magical world you don't need Aidon by your side to have the courage to deal with lawbreakers. *That* will have as much impact as you making Marius pay for what he's done."

Aidoneus closed the distance between us and cupped my cheek. "I can't allow you to go in alone. It's too much for me to handle."

Selene raised her hand. "I know I haven't been involved in all that many fights, but Layla has been training me. I can kick ass when needed. I'll go with you so that the shifters don't cause more problems with the vampires."

I turned to the side and smiled at the witch that had come to my door as a ghoul and become an important part of our little family. "I know you can protect yourself and me." My gaze shifted back to Aidon. "Will that work for you? You can storm the place with Layla and Tseki if we aren't out in fifteen minutes."

Aidoneus pressed his forehead to mine. "You're going to be the death of me, Queenie."

He didn't like everything I did, but he would never stop me from doing something. It made me love him even more than I already did. I'd been on my own for a while now and no one was going to come in and tell me what to do or how to do it. I'd rid myself of the asshole that spent twenty years treating me like I couldn't do anything right, and I would never allow it again. Aidoneus respected and trusted me enough not to go there.

I smiled up at him. "At least you'll die a happy man."

Aidoneus picked me up and swung me around in a circle. "The happiest."

He stopped spinning and pressed his lips to mine, kissing me like our lives depended on it. Stella and Layla catcalled us while Nana told us to take it to my room. I didn't care. I came alive in a way I didn't know was possible when I was with Aidoneus.

CHAPTER 3

y legs were shaking the closer we got to Insomniacs. When we reached the nautical shop near the alley to the vampire bar, Aidoneus squeezed my hand. Then he pressed his mouth to my lips. I smiled up at him, making a mental note to visit the store for the sextant that was still behind the register.

Turning to Selene, I smiled at the witch. "Are you ready for this?"

Selene took a deep breath. "Absolutely. I've practiced the sun spell you told me about. Although, I only plan on using it if I want to incinerate some bloodsuckers. Marius has shown we can't threaten like Fiona and her friends did."

I chuckled; happy she was already focusing her intent. The vampires had shown me previously that we had to act fast if they attacked. It was the only thing that would save us. "Don't hesitate if anyone makes a move for your throat."

Her smile had a wicked edge to it. "I won't. I'm primed and ready."

Aidoneus eyed the staircase with a scowl. "We will be up here. I'm coming in if I get the slightest hint of a problem."

My heart swelled with love for the god. He was trusting me to handle this shit on my own. It felt wonderful to have such a powerful man have total faith in me.

I nodded before heading down the stairs, glad that they weren't icy like they were on my last visit. The red door at the bottom of the stairs was far more ominous after the events in New Orleans with the vamps. The blacked-out windows and the faint strains of music only added to the creepy ambiance. I leaned into Selene when her eyes landed on the guy standing in the doorway. "Stay close."

She moved closer and shifted her gaze from the bouncer at the door to the dance floor that was barely visible in the dim lighting. Selene moved even closer as we walked into the club proper, where it opened up and had tables and chairs circling the dance floor. The place wasn't packed, but there were more people than there had been on my last visit. The warmer weather always brought more people out and about. It appeared that applied to the undead, as well.

Off to the right was the long wooden bar with a dozen stools in front of it. The setup was like any other place, with liquor on shelves behind the same bartender as last time. She looked up at me, narrowing her eyes. I kept my head tall and my heart steady. These vampires had pissed me off, I couldn't be frightened of them this time.

Selene snorted as she looked around. "This place couldn't be any more cliché, with red velvet draping the walls."

The room went silent, so the only noise that could be heard was the music that was shaking the windows. I wanted to smack her and tell her to watch her words, but I kept myself under control as I scanned the area for the hallway that I'd been dragged down last time.

With the focus on us, I noticed several mundies that looked drunk. Their eyes were glassy, and their expressions let me know that being fed on wasn't painful like I had assumed. Some of them had that satisfied smile you got after a really good orgasm. The thought made my stomach turn with nausea.

Where the hell was that hall?

"Pleiades, bitch," a female vampire snarled at me.

Selene and I continued across the dance floor. I had to grab Selene's arm when she stopped. She was shaking like a leaf when I touched her. I understood her fear. It was almost impossible to ignore the feeling that you were flailing in the middle of the ocean with sharks circling. Some of the color had drained from Selene's face, and I could see the pulse pounding in her throat. *Great, nothing like chumming the water and sending the sharks into a frenzy.* I forced Selene to keep moving with me. I had to look like I knew what I was doing.

Focusing on finding the hall, I missed the vampires rushing us from behind. A hard body slammed into me and sent me flying across the wooden dance floor. My shoulder hit someone a few feet away. It saved me from hitting the wall, but served me up as an appetizer into the waiting arms of another vampire. My mind zeroed in on fighting the vampires, and my body went on autopilot. I'd been in more fights than your average bouncer at a popular New York nightclub since Hattie gave me her magic months ago. It served me well when I faced the assholes of the magical world. Unfortunately, my ability to focus and cast spells wasn't as automatic.

I tried to bend and reach for the dagger Sebastian had made me right after I became Pleiades. It had saved my life more than once. The arms wrapped around my torso refused to loosen, so I used a tactic I'd learned in self-defense classes in college and rammed my elbow back into the vampire's stomach.

A laugh in my ear was followed by fangs slicing into the flesh of my neck. I froze for a split second, like a deer caught in the headlights. My fear was replaced by anger. One arm went behind me. I clawed at whatever I could reach. The guy yanked his head away from me, tearing my neck in the process.

The sharks had gone into a full frenzy, with my blood streaming down my skin. The vamps were all trying to get past one another to reach me. They were somewhat mindless and fought each other in the process. It made it possible for me to grab my dagger and swing it at the vampire behind me.

The blade sliced through his neck as he came after me again. I had been able to keep my fear in check until I looked at his face. Time seemed to stand still. In the moment before my steel separated the skin of his neck, his eyes had turned red, his upper lips had curled back to reveal his fangs, which were dripping with blood, *my* blood. His expression would haunt me for months to come.

Time resumed, and hands grabbed me. I kicked out and spun around, breaking the hold on me while searching for Selene. My heart raced faster when I couldn't find her. A woman smiled at me, at the same time a guy dressed in a dark blue suit plunged his fangs into my forearm. My dagger was yanked out of my hand by the woman. My heart stopped as I stood there, weaponless, in a room full of vampires attacking me.

My knee lifted and slammed into the guy feeding from my arm. The loud snap of a breaking bone made me laugh. A fist collided with my face. I expected the bright red nails on the end of that hand to scratch my eyes out, but they didn't. Mainly because I kicked the vampire in the gut and sent her flying into a couple of her friends.

A bright flash of light to my right made several of the undead scream. The sun blazed to encompass that half of the room for no more than two seconds, but it was enough to make a handful of vampires burst into flames while those closest to me grabbed at their faces.

The smell of burning hair filled the room while I scanned for my dagger. I thought I heard the woman drop it, but couldn't be sure. The stench of burning flesh followed, making bile rise to the back of my throat. I gagged and covered my mouth with the back of my hand.

I shouldn't have let myself be distracted by the smells around me. The screams I could deal with, and I thought I was better at handling nasty scents after twenty years of working as a hospital nurse.

A chair hit my side, and I went down at the same time Selene rose with a cry. She flung charred bodies off of her, then looked around. The rage on her face was enough to freeze most beings. The vampires closest to her were too busy wailing in pain. Their skin was blackened, blistered, and sloughing off in places.

"Do the sun spell again," I shouted to her. I couldn't recall the words at the moment or I would have helped her.

Selene's eyes went wide as her hand wrapped around mine. She had cuts and bruises all over her face and her top was torn open, revealing fang marks on her upper breast. "Trying," she gritted through her teeth.

My head dipped once in response before I pulled my arm away, then twisted and ducked from the claws coming at me. A bottle of vodka slammed down on the top of my head. Glass shattered and I'm pretty sure it cut through the skin of my scalp. The sting that followed a second later confirmed that suspicion.

"That's a waste of good alcohol. If you're going to waste it, I'll take it off your hands," I told the vampire as I whirled on her. I grabbed the blonde ponytail and swung her around.

"Fuck you, bitch," the woman shouted at me as she clawed my hands to shreds.

My grip on her slipped as I was hit from both sides by large bodies. They weren't trying to knock me down. They seemed focussed on restraining me. I lay there with two big bodies holding me down. I squirmed and bucked and fought, but couldn't budge them.

I closed my eyes and tried to focus my intent on the sun and recall the spell. A hand at the back of my pants made my eyes shoot open at the exact same second my blood froze in my veins. "Oh, hell no."

Protect yourself. Through the sheer terror coursing through me, I ignored the rip of fabric and focused on a bubble surrounding me. "*Protego,*" I shouted.

My magic burst from me. It had been building right under the surface, waiting for me to call on it. The power rippled out and circled around me. Shouts in my ears were followed by the pressure lifting off me.

I surged to my feet, the two halves of my shirt falling to the floor. Thankfully, my bra didn't go with it. My pants were loose but not falling off and I was too busy staring at the sight of two men missing their hands. I was fairly sure I knew what the two of them had intended for me, and it only made me madder.

I called my witch fire to me and bounced balls of purple fire in the palms of my hands. The vampires waved their stumped wrists around, sending blood flying everywhere. Chaos had descended on the club and vampires were fighting each other at the same time Selene was battling a group of them.

She threw balls of electricity at chests and heads as she spun in a circle like she was in a washer on the spin cycle. A feminine scream filled the air before a woman flew at me. I tossed the fire in my palms at the two writhing on the floor. They burst into purple flames.

I braced myself as I watched the woman get closer. Fire

coated my hands as I caught the vampire by her shirt. I willed my flames to spread across her chest and to her long black hair. She fell to the ground, and I kicked her into the group around Selene.

A hand tangled in the back of my shoulder-length brown hair and yanked. I couldn't move without losing chunks of hair. My eyes traveled down, and my vision went red, when they landed on a tall, slender man with pale skin and slicked back dark blond hair that stood at the corner of the dance floor smirking at me.

I shouted, trying to get at Marius. "You never should have sent those vampires after us in New Orleans." The fingers in my hair tightened around the strands, making my scalp burn.

Refusing to allow myself to be stopped by the hand now wrapping around my throat, I sneered at the head vampire. "You're going to be my example to your kind that no one messes with me or breaks the rules in my territory."

Marius waltzed toward me slowly with a smile on his face. "I don't think so. You've made this easy for me by coming here."

The door to the club burst open, making everyone look over. My heart leaped in my chest when I saw Aidon stalk inside, followed by Layla and Tsekani. The holds on my throat and hair disappeared so suddenly that I fell forward. I caught myself on the back of a chair.

"You okay, Queenie?" Aidoneus's eyes never left Marius's as he spoke to me.

The bar was a mess. Tables overturned. One wall of the red velvet was engulfed in purple flames. Chairs were also broken and burned. Glass littered the floor and Selene was panting as she held a vampire by the throat.

I glanced down at my bra, then gestured to the two charred lumps on the floor. "I was just informing Marius that he is going to be my message to the vampire world that attacking me and breaking my rules is a big mistake."

Aidoneus cracked his knuckles and grabbed the closest vampire, lifting him into the air. He tossed the guy at Marius, who jumped to the side. "I'd be happy to drive the message home."

I rolled my eyes and shook my aching head. Blood was dripping down the sides of my face and I was covered in bites, but I wasn't letting him do this. "I've got Marius, Yahweh. If you can keep the witnesses from running, that would be great. My message can't be delivered without them." There was no doubt by what I said that I planned on killing Marius.

The head vamp had gone even paler than was typical for him. His color came back when he saw Aidon nod his head in agreement. He was once again underestimating me. I loved when they did that. My stomach churned as I realized I had no choice but to kill the head vamp. Killing others hadn't gotten any easier for me over the months, even if making the decision to do so had been a simple one.

Layla and Tsekani grabbed vampires and shoved them into chairs at the edges of the dance floor. Marius removed his jacket and handed it to one of the vampires. He said something to the guy in another language. It made Aidoneus snarl and several of his people move to the edge of their chairs.

"You will not make it out of this building alive if she dies," Aidoneus snarled at the head vampire.

I threw my head back and laughed. "You're one of those dumb, smart bad guys. You tried to get your vampires ready for when you kill me, and didn't think a *god* that has lived thousands upon thousands of years and has learned every language spoken would know what you were saying? You've earned a gold star for stupid."

Marius screamed at me and came running at me with his fists clenched. I dodged to the side and ducked. One of his hands came back around faster than I expected and sliced through the back of my shoulders. There was pressure for a split second before a loud pop sound filled the room. White-hot pain seared me as the flesh was separated.

My witch fire was in my hand as fast as the thought crossed my mind. I didn't have time to figure out how he'd gotten past my protection spell. He was running circles around me, inflicting small cuts as he went.

At first, it seemed like he was simply being a pest until I realized he was trying to weaken me. My fire balls missed him because he was moving too fast. After what felt like the hundredth pass around me, I stopped trying to hit him with my flames and started counting the seconds it took him to complete the circuit around me.

I needed my dagger. Using magic was bound to hurt one of my friends, or Aidon, who was pacing back and forth in front of me, so I searched the floors for the weapon while I counted and waited.

Silver glinted out of the corner of my eye from beneath one of the overturned tables. I threw myself toward the weapon the second Marius passed me. I skidded across the sticky floor. The knife was just out of reach.

Marius dove on top of me, sending me sliding across the floor. His weight made moving across the hard surface even harder. I'd bet my next paycheck I would be covered in friction burns across my torso. The one thing he did for me, aside from making the injuries he'd inflicted on my back open even wider, was to make it possible to grab the dagger. My fingers curled around the hilt. I flipped over and swung the hand holding the knife.

I watched the tip slide into the side of his neck and dragged the blade down as I tried to pull myself out from under him. There was a good chance I'd hit his carotid artery, and I didn't want his blood mixing with mine.

He dropped to the floor where I had been while Aidoneus rushed to help me up. I leaned on him to keep myself upright. I snarled down at Marius, who opened and closed his mouth while blood gushed from his wound.

I kept the bile at the back of my throat when I lifted my gaze to his vampires. "Go and spread the word about what happens if you turn against me or mine or break the rules. I will have no mercy for anyone."

I inclined my head to Layla, Tsekani, and Selene. They backed off of the watching vampires, who all stood up and took off out of the club.

Aidon took off his shirt and pressed it to my back. His jaw was clenched, and he stared at me for several long seconds. "That won't kill him, Queenie. You will need to pierce his heart or remove his head."

Bile choked me, and I coughed into my hand. "Can you do it for me? I'm pretty sure I'm a second away from passing out."

Tsekani walked over with his hand partially shifted. "I've got Marius, Phoebe."

Aidon swept me into his arms. "And I've got you, love."

I smiled at him as my eyes slipped closed and the adrenalin faded. Everything around me vanished as I gave into sweet oblivion.

CHAPTER 4

I grunted as the car hit a hole in my driveway. "Holy crap, that burns. So much for luxury cars handling the road better."

Selene chuckled a pain-filled sound. "This little trip cured me from my desire for a car like yours, Aidon. I'm going on a shopping spree with the money I've already saved as soon as I feel better."

Aidon squeezed my hand as he continued down the drive to my house. "Clio should be here soon, Queenie. You both have some nasty wounds. Next time, I go in with you."

Layla snorted from the backseat next to Selene. "Our focus needs to be on making sure she stays alive. I can't believe you took down a master vampire by yourself, Phoebe. That was pretty badass and gives me a lot more confidence that you can take care of yourself."

Aidon parked the car. "With luck, news of that fight will spread throughout the magical world. That should curtail weaker enemies."

"Like Brody," Tsekani said from the back of the vehicle. He'd only recently come out of the depression he'd been in since the holidays. I missed his presence in and around the house. "I'm glad you didn't do this before he showed his true colors. He might have continued fooling me."

"He cleared the way for you to find your mate, Tseki. Let's get you two inside." Layla opened her door when Aidon parked, then went to Selene's side.

Tsekani climbed out behind the two of them. "Damn right. But those are thoughts for another day. I can't believe that asshole destroyed the Burberry top I got you for Yule. It took me weeks to find a shirt that didn't make your brown hair look drab."

I groaned when Tseki wrapped his arm under my knees. The movement twisted my back, making the wound break open. Aidon's shirt was pressed to my back while I clutched a blanket that kept the wadded-up fabric against my back.

"I know you're trying to distract me. My hair is always fabulous," I told Tseki.

The dragon shifter winked at me as he carefully transferred me into Aidon's arms. "You're right, even those random hairs on your chin shine with health."

My laugh ended in a grimace and groan. "I'll arrange to have it waxed before I leave for North Carolina. Thanks for not letting me walk around with a beard, Tseki. I don't know what I would do without you."

Aidoneus pressed a kiss to my lips. "You don't have a beard, Queenie."

I snorted, knowing full well that Tsekani was right when he mentioned my chin hair. It was the only hair I wasn't worried about losing as I closed in on menopause. No matter what I did, there were always one or two hairs that continued to pop up along my chin.

"You're right, Yahweh. It's more like a teenage boy going through puberty," I corrected.

My front door flew open, and my daughter came running

to us. She stopped at the top of the steps with wide, frightened eyes. "Are you alright?"

Stella was a second behind her. "Thank God. I was just one minute away from sending Sully and his shifters after you."

I smiled at both of them, doing my best to contain the pain I felt. I didn't want to worry them more. "It looks worse than it is. Clio is on her way."

Nana waved us inside from the doorway. "Let's get you inside so you can tell us what happened."

Aidoneus walked inside the house and carried me to the living room where my mother was laying a blanket over the sofa. "I'll get you some tea. I made some muffins that will amplify Clio's healing magic."

"Thanks, mom. Though I'm not sure I can eat anytime soon." My stomach was in knots and churning with bile.

Aidoneus set me on the edge of the couch and tugged the blanket to fall from around my shoulders. "Can someone bring some clean bandages and some warm washcloths so we can clean her up?"

My daughter nodded and took off into the kitchen. Mythia flew past her, holding a basket. "I've got the first aid stuff, so all you need to grab are the wet cloths," the pixie called over her shoulder.

Thia set the basket on the coffee table, while Nana took a seat in her chair as Selene sat next to me on the sofa. Evanora, our resident ghost, appeared in the corner with a stern expression on her face. She looked Selene and me over. "You get into more fights than anyone I've ever known."

Nana rolled her eyes before stopping, pursing her lips. "This magical life comes with significant danger. Fate chose Phoebe because she can handle the crap that comes with it. Most would walk away the second they were attacked. But not a Dieudonne`, and especially not my granddaughter."

My mom returned and set a cup of tea in front of me, then took one of the wet rags from Nina. "What happened with the master vampire?"

My mom washed around my injuries while Layla and Stella did the same for Selene. As they worked, I told the group what had happened with Marius and his vampires while Mom and Aidon washed blood from my arms. When I finished, I was shaking, covered in sweat, and thought I was going to throw up. That had been a painful process, and they hadn't touched any of the injuries.

My daughter looked up at me from where she sat on the ground at my feet. "You just left a bunch of dead vampires there?"

Heat threatened to steal over my face as I lowered my head. Her question made me uncomfortable. My family was adjusting to the magical world, and we weren't used to the death and gore that seemed to rule it at times. Nina wouldn't understand why we left the club with the dead where they'd fallen. It was barbaric and cruel. Not to mention dangerous.

"I left the clean-up for them. It's part of them learning not to mess with me or mine. And don't worry about someone running across the scene. They already had a diversion spell around the place to keep mundies, not accompanied by one of them, away from the place." I couldn't look in my daughter's eyes as I explained, so I examined the bite mark on my forearm.

Stella ran a hand over the side of her neck. "Those creatures won't listen to anything but extreme violence, Nina. They nearly killed me and would have gotten your mom if she'd been a normal witch like the rest of us."

Nina scooted until she was pressed against my leg. "I'm the heir for my mom. I'll inherit her magic and position when she's gone. Do I have to worry about everyone coming after me, too?"

35

My heart cracked over the fear in my daughter's voice. I wanted to wrap her in my arms and promise she would be just fine. Doing so would be a disservice to Nina. She needed to know the dangers so she could protect herself, but not all right now. She was young, and I wasn't planning on going anywhere anytime soon. That gave me time to give her information in bits and pieces.

Cupping her cheek, I smiled down at her. "You will be safe as long as you stay in the house. It's the main reason I don't want you to come with us. And your safety is one reason I did what I did tonight."

Nina's forehead furrowed slightly. "If that's the case, then I shouldn't leave daily to go to school. I'm far safer not going."

I rolled my eyes. "Nice try, sweetheart. Demons aren't prowling the halls of your high school."

Nina glared at me and turned so she was no longer touching me, then crossed her arms over her chest. "That's where you're wrong. I'm pretty sure there are dozens of demons in my classes. Have you forgotten what a troll Jean-Marc was a few years ago?"

Nana laughed as she took one of the muffins my mom had placed on the coffee table. "Those boys only seem like monsters. They're teenagers, which I know is far scarier. You made friends with those kids from the Grey Crest pack. They can't be all that bad."

"And they'll help keep you safe," Layla added. "Enjoy this time while you can. Soon enough, you will be sitting in on board and coven meetings and being asked to make decisions when your mother is away."

The doorbell rang, saving me from Nina's freakout. Aidoneus was up and moving to the door before I could ask anyone to get it. Hearing Clio's voice successfully diverted a conversation that didn't need to happen right now. My body sagged in relief when I knew Clio was here to help us. I was a second from breaking down and crying. My back felt like it had been dipped into a deep fryer while my arm and neck felt like the worst toothache ever. Only between the throbbing the areas went completely numb.

"It's about time you took care of Marius," Clio said as soon as she walked into the living room.

I lifted one eyebrow. Aidon shrugged a shoulder. "I told you it would spread fast."

Clio chuckled. "Nothing stays secret for long. Word on the street is that you left an abattoir for the vampires. Bold move. I think killing Marius was enough of a message. Now, let's look at your wounds."

I gasped when she lifted Aidoneus's shirt from my back. I was certain all of the flesh was cooked and going to fall off of my bones. Bathing in lava had nothing on this agony.

"Aidoneus and Tsekani are going to burn the dead as soon as the vampires take stock." I met Aidon's gaze, grimacing, when Clio hit something on my shoulder.

Clio grabbed a clean square of gauze and a bottle from the bag she brought with her. "Master vampire injuries are much harder to heal than regular ones. This is going to be a painful process. Speaking of, who is taking over the clan here, now?"

My jaw clamped shut as jolts of fiery pain shot through my back. I tried to inhale and calm the pain. Unfortunately, breathing wasn't easy to do at the moment. "That's not my problem."

Clio pressed the damp gauze over the bite on my arm. "I'm going to take my time cleaning these before healing. We have time, where I know Kip didn't when she treated you, Stella. The next master should be your main concern. If the wrong vampire takes over here, you could have an even bigger problem."

"Ah!" I shouted when she rubbed the gauze over my neck. My vision went blurry and my heart raced even faster. "I have a dead body in North Carolina that I have to go and deal with. I don't have time to give the vampires right now. Besides, I'd bet they all fled Camden after my visit."

Clio grabbed a clean piece of gauze and added more of the potion to it, then ran it over my arm. "Don't kid yourself. Vampires will never leave here. Having a Pleiades attracts all sorts to our city. They see it as a gourmet buffet. Let me heal these, then I can move on to your back."

After cleaning the wounds, she placed her palms over first one bite mark and then the other. Warmth flowed from Clio and into me. Her energy was like a mountain stream as it worked its way through the bites and other minor cuts. The injury hurt exponentially for a couple of seconds before the skin started knitting back together.

Sweat dripped down my back, adding to the pain. I could breathe easier now that the bites and other minor scratches were healed, so I shook my head. "You should help Selene first. I know my back will take you more time and I don't want her suffering any longer than is necessary."

"I can wait. Let her help you first," Selene objected. "My injuries aren't as bad as yours are."

I growled at her. My mom interrupted what I was going to say. "Don't try to talk her out of this, you know how stubborn she can be."

"I'm not being stubborn this time. I need a freaking break before I puke." I placed a hand over my stomach.

Clio inclined her head before she moved to the other side of the sofa. "You had a lot of cuts to heal along with the bites. That couldn't have been pleasant. You might want to eat something to replenish your energy before I move to your back. That's going to take both of us and Aidon."

I accepted the muffin Aidon picked up for me. It was

banana nut, my favorite. I took a small bite and chewed while I considered my current dilemma. I was always faced with a choice of what to prioritize in this new magical life, so having to debate between this vampire mess and a dead body was nothing new.

The vampires would take some time to get themselves together, whereas the pack in North Carolina wouldn't be happy about me leaving a dead body with them for very long. Not to mention the woman and her family. They all deserved closure.

"I understand what you are saying about the next leader here," I said, going back to the unfinished conversation. "However, the dead elf needs to be dealt with first. Do you think the vampires will mobilize in the next few weeks?" There was no saying how long this would take. It could be fast, or it might take time.

Clio sighed as she cleansed Selene's wounds. "It won't take long for someone to fill the power vacuum left in Marius's wake. I believe the most powerful vampire left alive lives in New York. It won't take her any time to move her clan here and take over what is left of Marius' in the process."

"What's she like?" Aidon asked. He took a seat on the arm of the sofa and I leaned my head against his arm.

Clio put the soiled gauze on the table and held her hands over Selene's face to heal those injuries first. "Her name is Guinevere and she's a diva. Gets pissed if her crystal goblet doesn't shine. She likes the nightclub scene. Other than a rumor, I have no idea what she's actually like."

I had to believe Camden's rather boring nightlife, compared to New York City, would be a deal-breaker for her. "Our nightclub scene pales next to what she has now. Let's hope she decides to keep the clan there."

Clio chuckled as she finished healing Selene. As the

healer moved back in my direction, she gestured for Selene to move off the sofa. "I need Phoebe to lie down for this."

My heart skipped a beat as I sat up straight. Ignoring the increased pain, I grabbed Aidon's hand and, with his help, lowered my body to the cushions. I didn't trust my strength to get me down without making my back worse. My muscles were quivering and threatening to give out.

Flat on my stomach, I turned my head to watch what Clio was doing. The healer moved a bowl closer to her, then poured the contents of three vials from her bag into the receptacle.

Clio turned to Aidon. "After I clean the area, I need you to push your energy into me to overpower the master's venom. It's supercharged in those of Marius's status. The toxins won't want to give way easily. It will want to continue turning her into a bloodsucker."

"What?" My voice was a shriek as I pushed myself up off the cushion. My arms gave out as white-hot agony stole my ability to think straight.

Aidoneus ran a hand over my cheek. "Relax. You aren't going to become a vampire. All you need to do is take it easy."

I closed my eyes, took several deep breaths, then nodded. My lids flew open and my muscles all locked down when a cool liquid washed over the wound on my back. The cold tried to counteract the lava burning throughout the area. I swear the two forces were fist-fighting beneath the surface of my skin. I think I cracked a tooth, given how hard my jaw was clenched. Clio's gentle energy was wrapped around Aidoneus's wild power as it worked through me. I felt the moment their combined magic reached the wounds.

Aidoneus's power blasted the venom in me. I felt cells being pulled from my tissue and bloodstream. At that point Clio's power surrounded those cells, and her warmth was turned down several notches. Without being connected to me, the cells popped like bubbles. The action made me smell like a sewer. I wanted to turn my head and see if gas was leaving my body like a toxic cloud, because it sure as hell smelled like it.

A second later, the agony stopped, and Clio's power left me. Aidoneus's lingered and seemed to encompass me like an embrace. I reached for his hand as I sat up. I thanked Clio for her help, promising to follow up about the vampires after we returned. My mom walked her to the door as I stretched my back, making sure I had no lingering discomfort. It felt great.

Tsekani walked into the room and handed me a soft pink sweater. "I figured you would need a top. And this color will help improve your color. You haven't been this pale since you had to have surgery a while back."

"Thanks for making sure I look my best at all times," I told Tseki with a smile.

After pulling the sweater over my head, I picked up the muffin that I'd dropped earlier. I hadn't eaten more than a bite. Now that I was no longer in pain, I was hungry for more.

"Did Morgan text the travel plans?" I asked my mom when she returned a second later. I'd left my phone with her when I went to Insomniacs.

My mom nodded. "She sent the rental information and has the plane on standby. I told her you were dealing with Marius and weren't certain how long that would take."

Nina had moved from the floor to the recliner next to Nana, now that I was no longer injured and bleeding. "Are you going to see Emmie, Greyson, and Skylar while you're down there?"

I tilted my head to the side. "Yeah. I'd like to leave first thing in the morning, but I won't get to them right away. I'll visit the three of them and Jean-Marc when I get a chance. I know Fiona said Greyson is eager to meet a dragon shifter, so he'll probably ask you to shift, Tsekani."

Tseki pursed his lips. "We will need a lot of space for me to shift. Before that, though, I'd better go pick up my dry cleaning and get packed. I can't go on a trip without my Tom Ford pants. They go perfectly with my Ferragamo loafers."

Aidoneus lifted a brow. "You'll want to pack clothes fit for fighting. We should assume that we will run into issues along the way."

Tseki nodded. "I've already thought of that and have planned those outfits. You can't go to dinner in dirty leathers, though."

I laughed and shook my head at Aidoneus. Trying to understand why Tsekani was concerned about that was not worth the debate. He had impeccable taste and always looked good. He was also there by my side, fighting when I needed him, so I figured he could focus on whatever he wanted.

CHAPTER 5

*M*y previous life flickered across my mind like a reel on one of those social media sites. You know, the short videos where images of various scenes rotate rapidly? Those drive me crazy when I come across them because I want to examine the pictures making up the clip.

That wasn't the case as Aidoneus drove us from the private airport and through the town I'd lived in half of my life. I'd gone to college, gotten married, had kids, and made my career here. And yet, the only part of that life that remained were my kids and my best friend, Fiona, along with her children.

Nostalgia hit as we turned down the street where the hospital was located. "That's where I worked for nearly twenty years. It looks the same, but different at the same time."

"It's you that's different, Queenie. I imagine it seems so much smaller than it used to for you," Aidoneus said as he continued past the massive five-story building.

I cocked my head to the side and looked over at him. "That's precisely how it feels. It's the magic in me, right?"

He shot me a smile. "Very good."

I shrugged my shoulders. "It makes sense. The power always feels so much bigger than me. Like I'm floating in the middle of the ocean."

Tsekani stuck his head between the front seats. "We're stopping by the house first, right?"

Aidon shook his head from side to side as he followed the directions and jumped on the freeway. "No. We're going straight to the pack so Phoebe can examine the body. Any magical trace left behind is degrading and we've already had to wait a day and a half."

Tseki ran his hands down his shirt and looked himself over. "Thank the gods my clothes aren't rumpled. I haven't seen Jay in years. The last thing I want to do is look like something the cat dragged in."

Stella pushed his shoulder from the seat next to him. "As if you could ever look less than perfect. Is Jay a *special* friend?"

Tseki's smile vanished. "Jay and I have never been an item. Myrna experimented on him when he was a young man and I helped him escape her lab. We reconnected when Hattie rescued us and we've been friends ever since."

There was a story there, but by the tone of his voice, he wasn't welcoming further discussion. I knew Myrna had created him and Layla by nefarious means, but I'd never asked more about that time in their lives.

"That woman was a vile being who got what she deserved. Now we're on the case of another killer. If it's a demon, you can find them, right Aidon?" Stella asked as she pulled out her mirror and touched up her makeup.

"There are demons in the area, but none of them feels very powerful." Aidon held up a hand as he took the exit. "And before you ask, there aren't that many of them. You don't need to worry about the safety of Jean-Marc or Fiona's kids."

We were approaching the outskirts of town and getting close to the pack's land. "I assume the pack here will have a similar setup to the one in Camden. Is there anything I should know?"

"Almost all packs are designed around a central building that houses their meeting place where they share meals, have parties and gatherings, and have their medical clinic. Jay's pack is no different," Tseki explained.

"Makes sense," I replied as I watched the scenery outside the window while organizing my thoughts. *"Tarja. Are you there?"*

"I'm here Phoebe. Have you encountered a problem?" Tarja's voice in my head was as strong as if she was in the same room as me, even though she stayed home this time. We hadn't wanted to risk her in the event she was pregnant.

She'd been very tight-lipped about her time with Zephyrus in Stuleros, the familiar realm. All seven familiars had spent time there after the other Pleiades and I cleansed it of the Tainted energy with the goal of mating. They would repopulate the world with familiars for witches. Needless to say, I was anxious to hear if she was expecting kittens, or not.

"No. I just wanted to run through my plan with you again," I told my familiar.

"You are ready for this. This isn't a new situation for you, so you don't need to be worried. When you examine the body, cast the same spell you did on Kendal. It will help you determine the nature of the elf's death."

I silently thanked Tarja and drifted back to the others right as Aidoneus parked the vehicle behind what looked like houses. We got out and made it a couple of feet when we found ourselves surrounded by men and women all dressed alike in jeans and flannel shirts.

Tsekani walked up to a guy with short brown hair and green eyes. "Jay. It's good to see you."

Jay reciprocated the greeting. "It's been too long, friend. This is my alpha, Kason. Kason, this is Tsekani, the dragon that saved my life."

Kason inclined his head to Tseki. "I've heard a lot about you." The alpha turned to me, Stella, and Aidon. "One of you is the current Pleiades. I didn't realize how powerful your kind really were. I've never felt anything like it."

I dipped my head a fraction. "I'm Phoebe, the Pleiades. And this is my best friend, Stella. And my mate, Aidoneus, it's likely Aidon's power you feel seeing as he's a god."

Kason's eyes widened for a fraction of a second, then narrowed as he scanned Aidon from head to toe. After taking his measure, the alpha bent at the waist and bowed to the man I loved. It was odd to see. I often forgot who and what Aidon was.

"We are pleased to welcome a god of?" Kason's words trailed into a question.

Aidon placed a hand over his stomach and repeated the gesture. "I am a god of the Underworld. Hades is my father, and the pleasure is mine. Thank you for handling the victim for Phoebe. It allowed her time to deal with a pressing issue before coming here."

One of Kason's eyebrows went to his hairline. "The massacre she perpetrated at Insomniacs is all the talk. But they left out that she had help from a god."

Aidoneus glared at the alpha and took a step toward the guy. "That's because I wasn't involved in any way in the culling of that asshole and his minions. She did that all on her own, so you should watch yourself."

I moved forward and put my arms up at the same time Kason lifted his hands, palms out. "I meant no offense. I just assumed you helped her. If I had a mate, I'd never be able to let her do something like that without me. You have more restraint than I do."

The tension that sparked between the two men, threatening an all-out brawl, decreased considerably when Aidon chuckled and dropped his shoulders. "It's called faith in her strength and honoring the woman I fell in love with. She wouldn't be that person if I ran over her decisions and did everything for her. I much prefer a powerful woman that won't hesitate to put me in my place."

Kason laughed with Aidon. "Noted. I admit the way you say that makes me rethink my position. Not that it's an immediate concern of mine. Here, let's show you the victim." The alpha started for the space between the closest houses, which was where they'd come out to greet us.

We walked through the tight space into an area bustling with kids playing and adults doing various chores. There were several men and women sitting on porches with computers in their laps, as well.

The homes surrounded a large structure that looked like the product of a house and a church coming together. A wood deck wrapped around the entire main building. Right away I knew it was the meeting place Tsekani talked about.

I wasn't surprised when Kason passed the park area and garden and went up the stairs to the main structure. The alpha gestured to the activity around us. "Welcome to the Darktail pack. We discovered the victim's name was Edraele."

Kason opened the French style doors and gestured for us to enter. The space inside looked like a rustic banquet hall. It was large and open but had a warm, cozy feel to it. The walls were stained wood with heavy metal ornamentation. There were also pictures of full moons on the walls, along with an intricate metal piece of art. It was a D that had a tribal wolf's head integrated into its structure.

The tables throughout the room had live edges. The tops

were worn and scarred. They were works of art and currently being used as classroom desks. The adults were inside teaching the kids topics like math and English. It was a poignant reminder that while they might not be mundies, they still had the same needs.

"Have the elves been notified?" I asked, refocusing on the matter at hand.

Kason nodded as he led us to a hall on the left side of the building. "I called as soon as we brought her here. Don't worry, I explained to Tsarra, their local leader, that she needed to keep her distance when she identified her so you could conduct your investigation and locate her killer."

I inclined my head, but was focused on the room beyond the door he'd opened. It was set up like a miniature medical clinic with glass-fronted cabinets containing various supplies, from bandages to sutures to medications and potions. There were four hospital beds separated by curtains and monitors at the head of each one.

My focus zeroed in on the bed hidden behind the closed curtains. Magic flowed throughout the room. It held an earthy feel but wasn't as wild as that of the shifters around me. I hadn't been able to feel it until Kason opened the door. I wasn't familiar enough with elf magic to determine if that was her, or something else.

I sent out feelers before entering the space and picked up tendrils of the wild magic I associated with shifters. There was nothing off there. The other signature was weak, yet lively. I'd bet this woman liked to laugh and have a good time. I didn't pick up any ill intent, either.

Entering the room, I headed for the bed that was shielded. "I can feel her energy in here. She was a happy person."

Kason joined me. "That's precisely what Tsarra said about

her. She didn't understand why Edraele would be targeted. She didn't have any enemies."

Aidoneus put his hands on my shoulders, offering support for a task that was already breaking my heart. "Murderers rarely have an adequate reason. You should hear some of the pathetic excuses I've heard over the years."

My stomach roiled and my mind whirled. "Setting an example seems like it would fall into that category."

Aidon pressed his lips to the top of my head. "If you hadn't stopped Marius, he would have continued condoning the death of innocents, and come after you and those you love. There is no better reason than protecting others and stopping evil."

He was right. I knew it and reminded myself of that. The guilt that had threatened to overwhelm me a moment ago passed in seconds. I clenched my jaw as I pulled the curtain back. Stella sucked in a breath next to me. "Oh my. Poor thing."

I swallowed the bile that pummeled the back of my throat like a punching bag. Edraele had been chopped with some kind of a blade, like a knife or a sword. There were gaping wounds on her neck and chest and one of her pointed ears was missing. Blood matted her white hair and her eyes were the grey color of the dead. It was hard to tell their precise color anymore.

Placing a hand to my stomach, I moved closer. "I assume you gathered any evidence from her body," I said to the pack alpha. "I'd like to look at that next."

Kason nodded. "We have it in a box for you to take with you. For what it's worth, there was nothing out of the ordinary. Our scientific equipment is limited to microscopes and incubators. We don't have anything that can analyze DNA or determine if there was foreign matter on her."

I hadn't thought about that. "Given the nature of the case, I doubt we will find the killer by mundane means."

Stella walked to the other side of the victim. "I agree with you, Pheebs. This death screams magical to me. I can't explain why, but the weapon was no ordinary blade."

"Your instinct is telling you the same thing as mine is me. Alright, I'm going to look for any magical signature that was left behind." I took a deep breath and concentrated on my desire to get a sense of the magic behind this and overcome any blocks in my path. *"Revelare residuus magicae et obstructiones."*

Electricity shot from my hands like it had the first time I used this spell. Those sparks flew from me to Edraele. I knew it wouldn't set her on fire from experience, but I was still holding my breath as they hit her. I forced my breathing to remain even and measured while I focused on my intent.

There was no creepy-crawly sensation this time. What hit me was a pleasant warmth, like I was sitting outside on a moderate spring day. I gasped when a thousand wasp stings followed that sensation. It wasn't all that painful. What made me take notice was the underlying emptiness. *Whoever wielded this weapon had no say in their actions. It was feeding something else.*

I had no idea what prompted that thought. Those stings started making me tired. It felt as if my energy was being repressed. Part of that feeling was because of the enchantment. Last time I'd wanted to lie down and take a nap, as well.

Reaching out, I tried to grab hold of that magical thread. Elemental magic was sent back at me. I would have thought it came from the elf, but there was something more underneath it. It was whatever had killed her. Whatever had been used carried more power than I'd ever felt in a weapon.

Ending the spell, I placed a hand on Edraele's head. "Can

you call Tsarra and let her know they can pick Edraele up? I don't have answers for them yet, but I am working on it. I have a couple of signatures to look for and will not stop until I discover what happened."

Kason stepped away as Jay carried a box to the table set up against the opposite wall. I hadn't seen it until that moment. My focus had been on Edraele. Aidon grounded me when he put his hand on my back. It was exactly what I needed at that moment to continue. The spell I'd just done had taken it out of me and it wasn't possible to take a nap at that moment.

Stella lifted a plastic bag from inside and held it up. "Perhaps there will be something here we can use to scry for the killer."

I nodded my head, once again grateful I had Stella by my side. Two heads were better than one and the two of us complimented each other wonderfully. "We will take the box since that process is far more involved."

"Tsarra will be here momentarily," Kason said as he returned to our group. "She would like to thank you."

Butterflies took flight in my stomach. I kept shifting through the bags and noticed a cigarette butt in one. I hoped it was from the perpetrator because it would lead us to him better than anything else we had.

My head snapped up when silence suddenly descended on us. I scanned the room and didn't notice anything. I opened my mouth to ask when I realized the conversations in the main hall had stopped, as well.

The earthy energy preceded the local elf leader before she entered the room. The tall slender woman looked regal in her dark blue silk pants, white button down and low heels. Her long red hair was braided over one shoulder. She inclined her head to me. "You must be Phoebe."

Shocked that she knew I was the Pleiades, it took me a

second before I repeated her head movement. "Yes. It's a pleasure to meet you. I just wish the circumstances weren't what they are. I am sorry for your loss and want you to know I will be doing everything in my power to capture the person responsible."

Tsarra's blue eyes filled with tears as her gaze shifted to Edraele. "The elf community is prepared to assist in any way you might need. Many want to be involved but I have assured them their need for vengeance could inhibit the investigation."

"That's for the best. I will reach out if there are items that we need help with. What your community can do in the meantime is ask questions about Edraele. They shouldn't limit their questions to your kind. They have the connections here that I don't and will be more likely to get people talking. If they can find even one person that witnessed Edraele's attack, it will help us. Every detail can be helpful," I explained.

"I've already given those precise directions to my people. If you will excuse me, I must prepare Edraele for transport." Tsarra bowed to me then gestured to a blonde guy standing in the doorway. He was taller than her and just as skinny.

The two approached Edraele and Tsarra took out a green sheet that looked soft as silk. The guy lifted Edraele as Tsarra spread the blanket on the table. After placing Edraele back on the surface, the two of them proceeded to wrap the fabric around the dead elf.

Tsarra left Edraele's head exposed so she could place silver coins over her eyes that were etched with runes. I wasn't familiar with what the symbols meant, but their placement wasn't surprising. Using coins over the eyes of the dead was common throughout history.

Once the silver was in place, Tsarra and the guy bowed over Edraele to say a prayer in elvish before wrapping her head in the green fabric. The respect and care they showed her touched me. Their ceremony was clearly important to them and so was Edraele.

Emotion burned in my throat as I exchanged numbers with Tsarra then we said goodbye. My heart was heavy as Tsekani and Aidon gathered what we were taking with us. This young woman didn't deserve what happened to her. I linked hands with Stella after we climbed into the car. My team and I were going to find out who did this and make sure Edraele was avenged.

CHAPTER 6

"hey look cozy," Stella whispered in my ear as we approached the table at my son's favorite restaurant.

Because we lived in the triangle in North Carolina, Jean-Marc had several choices of top universities to attend without having to go far from home. It meant he was comfortable in his environment when most college kids were adjusting to life outside their parents' home, living on their own, and navigating unknown territory.

I rolled my eyes at my best friend then waved to my son and his girlfriend. Emlyn's blonde hair was pulled into a messy bun and her brown eyes were lined with kohl. The way she looked at my son made it obvious how she felt about him. As Jean-Marc stood up, Emlyn smiled warmly at me.

"You look good, mom." Jean-Marc hugged me tight, reminding me of when he was a little boy and used to give me tight hugs as a way to try and get out of having to go to sleep at night.

He released me and wrapped an arm around Emlyn's waist. "You remember, Emlyn, right?"

I nodded then opened my arms and gave her a brief hug. "I do. It's nice to see you again. You recall my better half, Aidoneus and my best friend, Stella? And the best dressed among us, Tsekani?"

Emlyn chuckled as her cheeks turned pink and she plucked at her over-sized campus t-shirt that was loose over her skinny jeans. Next to Tseki's designer clothes and perfectly styled hair, Emlyn and I looked like little orphan Annie.

Tseki waved a hand in front of her. "You're a college student and have perfected the look, Em. Phoebe on the other hand retreated to that phase rather than make progress with her wardrobe. Teaching her a sense of style has become my second full-time job."

Emlyn's eyes went wide as she glanced between us. "You have that all wrong. Ms. Dieudonne` is beautiful and she dresses nothing like kids my age. Her outfits remind me of my mom and her friends."

One of Tseki's eyebrows rose to his hairline. "You've just made my case for me."

I punched him in the arm. "With the shit I face I need to be comfortable. Besides, you can't say I haven't upgraded what I wear. Now I wear expensive mom clothes. Simon Cowell looks good in his thousand-dollar-t-shirts, so it should work the same for me, too."

Jean-Marc motioned to the table. "I'm not sure that's how it works, mom. Regardless, you look better than you have in years. Happy."

I sat down, Aidon taking the seat next to me. After the morning we had with traveling, then examining Edraele, and dealing with the elves and shifters, lunch was a welcomed reprieve. For almost an hour I was back to being a normal mom of a young man on the cusp of adulthood. Jean-Marc might nearly be twenty, but he had a long way to go before he would be completely on his own. But the restaurant wasn't the best place to visit with my son. We couldn't have an open conversation. I kept the conversation on topics like his grades and how he liked his roommate before suggesting we take a walk through a nearby park so we could catch up without fear of being overheard.

Aidoneus twined his fingers with mine as I got out of the rental car. The park wasn't far but it was easier to take our vehicles the mile and a half down the road than traverse the busy street on foot.

Jean-Marc's hand reached for Emlyn then dropped back to his side. I patted his shoulder with my free hand. "How are you doing? With your magic and becoming depleted?"

Jean-Marc stuffed his hand into his pocket and pulled out an opalescent stone the size of a walnut. "I've got my lode-stone charged at all times. It's helped keep me level. Emlyn and I visit the ley line at the other side of this park regularly, so I can recharge it and avoid the urges."

Men aren't witches like women, but they can be warlocks or mages. Warlocks use the elements to fuel their spells while a mage is connected with the magic of the earth itself. Warlocks and mages need to remain near ley lines. Or visit a powerful area often to recharge their energy. Otherwise, they run the risk of giving in to the desire to steal it from others. It is only those regular infusions of energy that keep them from turning Dark. Needless to say, men are far more susceptible to becoming Tainted.

Emlyn moved closer to him, grabbing his hand. "He's gotten to the point that he recognizes the signs on his own now. I haven't had to mention he's getting low once since he was home last."

That had been a couple months ago and her reassurance settled a lot of my worry. "That's fantastic news! Have you discovered where your magic is centered? The earth, or do you draw from the elements?"

Jean-Marc grimaced as he guided Emlyn off the path and onto the lawn. "I think I'm damaged because of how we got our magic. I do both which Em has told me is not normal. The pixies also told me I'm more powerful than I should be as a man."

My mind immediately called out to Tarja. *"Please tell me there's nothing wrong with him."*

"That's not typical but your family hasn't followed what Hattie or I expected. We will take this one day at a time. He needs to practice with both styles and try to determine which is stronger. He will likely lean in one direction or another. None of this is a bad thing, just more proof of how special you and your family are."

My heart was in my throat as I thanked Tarja. I would have asked more but she sounded tired. It gave me hope that she had conceived her first litter. Shoving those thoughts aside, I relayed what Tarja had said about practicing his magic.

"He smells like the earth to me," Tsekani observed. "If I had to guess, I'd say you're more mage than warlock. Not that either name fits you. You deserve something better. It's a big deal to have a new type of magic user. I know, what about calling you the first *magius* or *esoti*. I personally like *esoti*. It has an exotic ring to it."

I shrugged my shoulders and looked at my son. "This is your call, Jean-Marc. You're the first and might be the only, but Tseki is right. You should have a name so others understand you better."

Jean-Marc rubbed the back of his neck with his free hand. "I like *esoti*. It fits and I don't have a better idea."

The trees were getting thicker around us, making me feel like we were back in the forest between Aidon's house and mine. Before I knew what was happening, a tiny pixie came flying out of the thickest part of the foliage and stopped a few inches from my face.

"Oh!" I stumbled back a step and Aidon caught me. My gaze scanned the park around us, hoping there weren't mundies nearby. "Well, hello. You surprised me."

Emlyn gaped at me and the pixie. "I can't believe they came out here like this. We always see them zipping through the canopies when we visit the ley line but they never get close."

Jean-Marc nodded and lifted a hand to the tiny woman. She had bright red hair and iridescent wings flapping as fast as a humming bird's. She wore black pants and a neon green top that made her skin glow. "Is there a mound in this park?"

The pixie made a squeaking noise before she bowed at the waist. "I had to come meet the new Pleiades. I am Pasna. Your reputation as a friend to our kind precedes you. Your son comes here often. He's a powerful man and not like anything we know."

Jean-Marc smiled and his chest puffed up. I knew my boy well enough to understand he appreciated being told he was unique. He introduced himself along with the rest of us. "No one like me has existed before. I'm an *esoti*, a combination of a mage and a warlock. I won't hurt you. I'd love to visit when I come here."

Emlyn's face creased with a huge smile as she practically bounced on her toes. "Oh my, this is such a privilege. I can't believe how much they're talking to us. My mom was surprised they had said anything to Jean-Marc before."

My forehead wrinkled as I took in what she was saying. "You mean pixies aren't a common occurrence in the magical world?"

Pasna shook her head, as did Emlyn. "Not at all," Em replied. "They can be seen if you're paying attention, but they don't take many chances given the technology today, so they stick close to their mounds where they're sure to be safe."

Pasna stuck her hands in her pockets. "Emlyn is correct. We are selective in where we create our mounds and where we spend time. We have to take care."

I shook my head from side to side. "I'm spoiled then because I have a mound on my property and one of my closest friends is a pixie, Mythia. I think Fiona's kids have a pixie living in their yard, too. You know they aren't that far from here."

Emlyn gasped while Pasna's face furrowed. The two spoke at practically the same time. "I'd love to see a pixie mound. I've always wondered about them," Emlyn said. "A pixie lives with a family in their yard around here?" Pasna asked.

I pointed to Emlyn. "You are welcome to visit Nimaha anytime you're free. Perhaps when the summer classes let out." Turning to Pasna, I inclined my head. "Yes, my friend who lives in England has pixies and one of them fell in love with her kids when they visited and returned to the states with them. I haven't seen them to know how it's going but I know they are keeping her safe."

Jean-Marc let go of Emlyn and pointed toward the parking lot. "We should go pay Greyson and the girls a visit to make sure they're doing alright. I'm afraid I haven't seen them in far too long."

Pasna dipped her head. "I will not keep you. Thank you for visiting with me. I hope to see you again."

"I will try to come back and see you. Before you go, I need to ask you for a favor. Can I tell the pixie living with my god children where you are located in the event that she is lonely and misses her kind?"

"We would welcome any friend of yours, Pleiades." Pasna

buzzed away after that. I watched her go and noticed a couple other pixies hiding in the trees.

I turned around and started for the vehicles. "Will you lead the way, Jean-Marc? I haven't been to their house before."

"No problem. It isn't far," he replied.

A band tightened around my chest at the same time a stone settled in my gut. I'd promised Fiona that I would look after her son and I hadn't done a damn thing. I was the worst friend alive. It wasn't as if the expense of flying was an excuse, either. I had my own damn plane.

My guilt was a huge thing that was impossible to ignore as we followed my son across town. Stella asked about Fiona's kids and I told her about Emmie, Skylar, and Greyson.

When we pulled up to the two-story grey country style home, I wondered what their neighbors thought about the yard. The grass was as green as a lime and as lush as carpet while the beds were full of vibrant, colorful flowers and thick shrubs. Not one of the homes in the area had this many plants without weeds or dead sections.

Jean-Marc got out of his car and went right up to the front door. I hurried to catch up. "Damn kid doesn't know it takes the rest of us a while to get out."

Stella chuckled. "That's teenage boys for you. Completely clueless."

The door swung open when we were halfway up the walk. It was then that I heard the yelling inside. Tsekani moved forward, shielding me. I pushed at his back. "It's Skylar, Fiona's daughter. We're okay."

My fierce dragon nodded and stepped aside. Together, we climbed the stairs and joined Emlyn and Jean-Marc as they entered the house. Emmie was shouting at Greyson about being a jerk.

"Auntie Phoebe, you're here. It's been too long since we've seen you," Skylar said as a greeting.

I embraced Skylar. "It's good to see you, Sky. What's going on between your brother and sister?"

Skylar sighed and gestured to the back of the house where I could see a kitchen table. "Greyson has been grumpy and tired, even though he's sleeping more and more. Emmie said he tried to attach to her magic and he thinks she's crazy because we literally know crap about our powers."

I winced. "I'd better go check that out." That didn't sound good. I quickly walked away without introducing everyone else. When I saw the red flames dancing across a pair of women's boots, I knew they were courtesy of Greyson.

"What is going on in here?" I called out as I entered the open space of the living room and kitchen. "Put out that fire before you burn down the house."

Greyson and Emmie both stopped arguing and looked my way. Emmie was the first to smile and rush toward me. "Auntie Phoebe! I'm so glad to see you."

I hugged her back then introduced everyone before I forgot my manners altogether. "I should have come sooner but life has been crazy since I was given my magic. You guys have changed as much as we have. We can discuss that in a second. First, I want to know the meaning of you burning your sister's shoes?"

Greyson ducked his head. "She's being a bitch."

Emmie opened her mouth to give an angry retort. I held up my hand. This was not like Greyson at all. He was a sweet boy and always kind. The anger he was showing right now seemed completely out of character and gave me the chills. It also raised suspicions about his current condition.

I prayed I was wrong about him being on the verge of Turning. It would be all my fault if that happened. I was closer and had promised Fiona to look in on her kids. Taking a deep breath, I gestured to the kitchen table. "Put that fire out and tell me more about what's been happening. Have you felt drained lately, Grey?"

"Like you can hardly lift your head in the morning?" Jean-Marc added. "Or maybe you've felt empty. Like there's nothing inside."

Greyson dipped his head before crossing his arms over his chest. Although, he did extinguish the red flames. "It's nothing I can't handle. I don't need lectures from you guys, as well."

"Sit down, so we can talk," I instructed before moving to the fridge. It was abysmally empty. Moving to Stella and Tseki, I pulled them aside. "Can you two go and grab some groceries while I chat with Greyson and the girls? They need everything you can imagine."

"No problem. Any allergies we should know about?" Stella asked.

I shook my head and hugged her before they left. Aidoneus was sitting at the table with the kids when I joined them. "They're getting food and supplies while we talk. Have you been using your lodestone, Grey?"

Greyson stared into my eyes and shook his head back and forth. "I haven't used it since my mom gave it to me. I thought she was overreacting and tossed the thing in the drawer. I'm not going to look stupid carrying the thing around. But I have gone to the ley lines to recharge."

"That's not enough," Aidon replied.

Greyson scowled at the love of my life. "Who are you to tell me what to do?"

I pinned Greyson with my mom glare. "He's my mate, but more importantly, he's a god and incredibly powerful. And he's been around a long time, not to mention he's your elder and you respect your elders."

Emmie leaned forward on the table. "See? He's not okay and he won't listen to me."

"Casting accusations like that will get us nowhere. Have you guys been practicing your magic so you can get a better handle on it?" I hated to come in and start dictating to them, but they needed to understand how things worked so they didn't accidentally set fire to something. Or worse.

Skylar shrugged one shoulder. "We try but we haven't been able to find a coven to learn with. The one we visited were all a bunch of old women and they didn't like Greyson at all."

Emlyn sucked in a breath. "That's not surprising. I've had similar problems. What if we formed a coven of our own? There would be five of us and I could use the practice."

Emmie scowled at the young witch. "How is that going to help? We don't know enough to help each other. That's the problem."

I wanted to ask if they'd spoken to their mom but held back. They'd had a big enough struggle accepting everything. "Emlyn grew up a witch. She can teach you the basics and help you learn control. You can't try more advanced spells before you're proficient with the basics. Not to mention, she can help you with easy potions."

Emlyn smiled at them. "I have a copy of my family's grimoire we can use, as well. This could be what we all have needed."

Emmie pursed her lips. "I'm willing to try. I can ask my mom to email us pictures from our family spell book, so we'd have that, too."

Greyson sneered. "I'm not a pansy. I can do this on my own." He pushed away from the table and stalked out of the room.

Emmie growled while Skyler chewed on her thumbnail. I sighed and pinched the bridge of my nose. I was way out of my depth here. My love for these kids was the only thing pushing me to continue. I'm ashamed to admit that if they were someone else's kids, I would have given my advice and left. Instead, I shoved Edraele to the side temporarily, so I could deal with Greyson and what he was going through.

CHAPTER 7

"*Tarja. Are you there?*" I sent the mental message to my familiar as I helped Stella put away the groceries.

Jean-Marc was trying to talk to Greyson, who was scowling at everyone with his arms crossed over his chest. Every now and then I felt his power brush up against mine. It gave me the creeps and made me worry about the fate of one of my best friend's children.

"*I'm here. What happened? You sound worried.*" Her voice was clear and strong, yet she sounded as if she had been sleeping again.

"*Weren't you listening?*" It wasn't like her not to be in the back of my mind when I was on cases like this. The only time she hadn't been there was when I was lost on Mount Batia and there was some magic blocking our communication.

"*No, I wasn't. I trust that you can deal with Fiona's children. And I was conserving energy. It seems I'm going to need it for the next two months.*"

"Oh my God! You're pregnant." Joy burst through me at

the thought. She could have up to twelve babies by the time fall rolls around.

"Who's pregnant?" Stella asked. "Tarja?"

My cheeks flushed. I hadn't realized I'd spoken out loud in my excitement.

"Yes, it seems Zeph and I were successful when we mated. Can we get back to the matter at hand?"

I nodded in response to Stella. Tarja could speak into everyone's mind when she was in the room, but this far that was limited to her and I. Turning my attention to my familiar, I felt a smile spread across my face. *"Congratulations, Tarja. I am happy for you. I have no idea how I need to support you through this, but I am here for you. I was reaching out to ask about Greyson's behavior. I'm worried about him."*

I thought through my observations for Tarja and watched Stella pause in putting fruit in the crisper to shiver and run her hands up and down her arms. I wanted to ask if Greyson was probing her but held my tongue then shifted my attention to Greyson.

"His aura is muddied. You are right to be concerned. He's on the cusp of Turning. All it will take is him grabbing for one of the wisps of powers dancing around him. You should call his mother and get him to a ley line to replenish his energy stores right away. Mages like him are more vulnerable when they are weak, as you know."

I knew that all too well. I thought of it often with regards to my own son. Pulling my cell phone from my back pocket, I thanked Tarja and dialed Fiona's number. Deciding I didn't want the kids to overhear, I went into their backyard.

Grams answered on the third ring. My heart was in my throat. She sounded groggy. Shit, I hadn't considered how late it was there.

"Hello Grams. I'm sorry for calling so late. I need to speak to Fiona." I spotted the pixie moving through the flowers along the back fence and smiled. I was still surprised the pixie returned with them.

"It's good to hear from you, Phoebe. Fiona isn't here at the moment. She went to Eidothea with Aislinn for the baby. Is there something I can help you with?"

"I don't want you to worry, but it's Greyson. He's struggling with his magic at the moment. I'm here at their house, but I thought Fiona should know."

I heard the rustling of fabric followed by the crash of ceramics on a hard surface. "You need to get him to the ley line right away. Hasn't he been using the lodestone? Why didn't those girls call and let us know?"

My heart was racing, making me as frantic as Grams sounded. Upsetting her more would not be helpful. I took a deep breath. "The girls just realized it. This is recent and I have time to help him. I will be taking him to a ley line and getting him the help that he needs."

"I am grateful you are there with him. Unfortunately, this is a lesson he needed so he doesn't fall prey to the urges of his magic and take his sisters down a path from which they can't be saved. You know how kids rarely hear their parents when they talk."

I chuckled. "My son listened because my familiar told him the warnings. However, if it was just me, he would have felt the same as Greyson and believed I was exaggerating. Don't worry, I will get him squared away. I'll call you tomorrow at a decent time and let you know how it went."

Grams thanked me for calling and said her goodbyes. Reentering the kitchen, I noted Greyson looked worse. Grabbing a couple of Cokes from the fridge, I took the seat next to him, handing one to him, then put the rest on the table.

"We need to get you recharged right away. You're close to Turning," I told Greyson.

He cracked open his Coke and shot narrowed eyes my way. "I am not that weak. I've got this under control."

Stella crossed her arms over her chest as she leaned against their island. "Is that so? Then tell me why you're feeling me up like I'm your prom date."

Greyson's cheeks flushed pink as his eyes flew open. "What? I'm not touching you."

I frowned, realizing he wasn't aware of what he was doing which made it even more dangerous. "Actually, your power is doing precisely what Stella described. It's seeking a source to replenish what it can't. It's going to get control of you and suck in magic from one of us before you can stop it."

Aidoneus slapped a hand on the table. "Sounds like we had better get moving then."

Greyson shook his head as he curled in on himself. "I can't leave yet. There's a midterm worth half of my grade in my statistics class in two hours. I can't miss it or I'll fail. That can't happen. My mom sacrificed to give us money for this house and tuition. I can't let her down."

My stress over making sure Greyson was alright, took a rocket through the roof and was on its way to the moon. It was suddenly hard to breathe as I thought about failing him and his mother. Part of me wished Fiona was on Earth, so we could shoulder the burden together, but she wasn't. She was in another realm and out of touch completely. I knew she would do whatever it took if the situations were reversed.

Stella smiled at Greyson. "You will break her heart if you steal from your sisters and become Tainted. There isn't a worse fate for our kind."

Skylar's lower lip trembled. "Can that really happen?"

I wanted to shield her from everything and tell her it would be alright. But that would be a huge disservice to her. "Given the way his magic is reaching out without his prompting, your brother is not far from that point. He hasn't visited the ley lines often enough."

Emmie sighed and grabbed Greyson's hand. "I wondered if you should have gone more and never said anything."

I held up a hand. "This is not the time for blame. We need to visit the more powerful ley lines so you can refuel yourself and charge your lodestone which means we need to take a trip to the mountains. I don't think this can wait. I'm happy to call your professor."

Greyson shook his head. "No, I don't want to wait. I spent the entire night studying and I'm ready to take it now. Isn't there anything you can do for me?"

"Have Jean-Marc give him his lodestone. He can take the power from it to get him through the test."

I jumped when Tarja's voice entered my mind. I hadn't expected it given her condition. *"Thank you for the advice. I would have given him some of mine. But I don't want you hanging out because I said something earlier. It's more important that you take care. You're expecting."*

Aidon's forehead furrowed as he reached for me. I gave him a smile letting him know I was alright. He inclined his head, twining his fingers with mine.

"I'm glad I did stick around. You should never give someone your power. It opens a door for them to take it all. The Pleiades power must be freely given. Always infuse it into an object for them to use. I should have told you this after you gave it to save Stella. That time was chaotic and I never revisited the topic. Then there was me, but our bond makes it possible for us to share. The same goes for Aidon."

"Stella would never steal from me. I trust her implicitly. Thank you for sticking around and letting me know. I'm fairly sure that would have become my go-to method of saving people."

I turned to Jean-Marc. "Would you be willing to loan

your lodestone to Greyson? If he can absorb the power from it, he will be able to get through his test."

Jean-Marc nodded his head then pulled the opalescent stone from his pocket. It twinkled in the light that came through the back windows. "Absolutely. I'd do anything for a fellow coven member. Not to mention a cousin."

My kids had grown up with Fiona's, so they were more like family than anything else. Greyson took the stone from Jean-Marc. His reaction was immediate. He shuddered and groaned as power flowed from the stone and into him. It heated the air around him with the speed the transfer occurred.

After several seconds, Greyson's color was better, the scowl left his face and he smiled at us. "Thank you, auntie. I didn't realize what an idiot I'd been."

I placed a hand on his arm. "That wasn't much power, so you need to be careful. We need to go to the site in the mountains as soon as you're done. I know there is one located there but not it's precise location. Do you know where it is, Emlyn?"

She sat up straighter. "I've never been there but I will do some research. I'd love if we could do it together." She said that last part to Emmie and Skylar. "It would be a great introduction to accessing magical information online."

The young woman was happy to form this coven. I imagined, having grown up in the magical world, it was hard being disconnected while away from home.

Stella straightened from the island. "Is that shared on a database? I'm looking for a way to expand my magical listings to more areas and attract new buyers."

One of my eyebrows went to my hairline. "You don't have time to expand, Stells. We're kept very busy with these cases."

My BFF rolled her eyes at me. "I've had an elf and a dwarf

ask if I was hiring any magical agents. This is something we can take worldwide. People everywhere need to find the right place to live and can't go to a standard agent for help. This would be incredibly successful if we have a network online."

Emlyn nodded her head and bounced in her seat. "That would be incredibly useful. Especially for witches, mages, and warlocks. I know if I were to marry someone like Jean-Marc or Greyson, I would want to find a place close to, or on, a ley line. It would save a ton of time if someone has already done the research."

Jean-Marc's face heated and he lowered his head. I smiled at my son. He assumed she was giving him a hint. It was amusing to see him squirm and a relief to know Emlyn wasn't hinting at wanting to get married. She was merely making a point.

"Let's meet up this evening so we can head to the mountain together."

The kids all agreed, then we left to go and investigate the items collected at the scene. As my mind shifted to Edraele, I wondered if this was the first death of its nature in the area.

I said goodbye to my son and his girlfriend and then got into our car. As Aidon pulled away from the house, I voiced my concerns. "I'm worried there have been more deaths in the area. We should look into that after we inspect the items collected at the scene."

"And after we take Greyson to get recharged tonight," Stella pointed out.

My to-do list never ended. Items seemed to magically be added before I accomplished even a fraction of what was on there. Normally, I shoved the list aside and focused only on the most pressing matters at hand, but I needed to make things like checking on the kids a priority. They might be adults but they still needed a mother figure in their lives. They weren't capable of handling everything on their own just yet.

CHAPTER 8

*W*e'd looked over everything the shifters thought to gather at the park where Edraele's body was dumped. The only thing we'd been able to discern with any kind of certainty was that she wasn't killed where she was found and that the weapon was likely either a dagger or an ax.

I was leaning toward a dagger or another knife with a short blade. Tsekani theorized it could also be an ax, saying Edraele's wounds were wider than those created by knives. Working in a hospital, I had experience with all sorts of wounds and knew they widened naturally once the skin was split. That didn't mean the weapon was bigger, but we couldn't rule it out.

An hour later, Aidoneus parked the vehicle in front of the local police department. "What's the plan here?"

I sat forward looking through the windshield. "I'm not entirely sure. I just want to know if there have been other deaths that might fit this modus."

Tseki touched a hand to his perfectly styled hair. "We need to make sure. Something tells me we are dealing with a serial killer here and if they are somehow targeting paranormals, we need to know about it."

My head snapped around and pinned Tseki with a glare. "What the hell do you mean the perpetrator is a serial murderer? There's nothing here to indicate that's the case."

Tseki lifted one hand in the air and gestured to his head and upper chest. "It's mostly a feeling in my gut. There's also the fact that she was dumped in the park and her wounds don't indicate someone that was caught up in a fury of emotions. There would have been more and she would have had defensive wounds. The culprit subdued her somehow."

Aidoneus climbed out of the driver's seat. "That's a good point and something to keep in mind. Right now, we need to get inside and talk to an official that can give us information."

The afternoon heat beat down on us as we walked to the entrance. The temperature in Maine was usually comfortable, even in the middle of the summer. That wasn't the case in North Carolina. The higher temps and humidity complicated matters.

Halfway across the parking lot a hot flash hit, making my blouse stick to my back with sweat. Tsekani leaned closer to me. "Are you having one of those flash things? Because you look like a skunk with that stripe down your back."

Heat went to my cheeks. "You never say something like that to a middle-aged woman. The correct response is to tell her she's shining like a beautiful beacon."

Tseki laughed and was still chuckling when we reached the door. Aidon bent and pressed a kiss to my lips. "You look good enough to eat."

The low growl of his words were enough to make me shiver. Coupled with his lips on mine and I wanted to rip his clothes off and have my way with him. Instead, I twined my fingers with his. "Later, if you're lucky."

He laughed as we took in the lobby. There were a couple of plastic chairs and three desks behind bulletproof plastic. I approached the only one that had someone behind it. The woman at the desk looked at me and then took her time getting to her feet.

This was not what I expected in a police station. On shows, there was nothing separating you from the receptionist who was typically another officer. This woman was not in a uniform.

The older woman pressed something. "How can I help you?" Her voice came through a speaker and made me think of how prisoners and their visitors communicated, except there was no phone.

I shifted my feet. "I'd like to talk to someone in homicide, please."

She pursed her lips and narrowed her eyes. "Do you have a crime to report? Or are you a family member of a victim?"

I had to fight a snarky retort. If that was how this woman talked to the family of someone that had been killed, she should be fired. Her tone couldn't have been angrier if she tried.

"No, we aren't here to report a crime." We needed to know if there was immediate concern about exposure of the magical world. I opened my senses and detected a faint magical signature but couldn't get a read on it.

"We need to speak to a detective, please." If I could talk her into letting us in the back, I might be able to pick something up.

She shook her head and glared at me. "I'm afraid that's not possible."

Aidoneus leaned on the edge of the window, which was barely big enough for a strand of hair. "We aren't here to cause problems. You want to call a detective to come and speak with us."

75

The woman's scowl vanished and her expression softened a fraction. I cheered his ability to manipulate mundane minds while I didn't think too much about how icky that was.

The receptionist grunted. "I don't think that's possible. You need to leave."

Aidoneus unleashed a smile that melted the panties of every woman in the vicinity. "You'd like to take us to talk to Detective Richardson."

The woman wavered on her feet before nodding and moving to a door set to the side of her desk. It was a victory as she opened the panel for us. She was stubborn and distrustful enough that I didn't think he would be able to convince her. Not everyone could be compelled. If a mundane had a strong enough mind, they could resist. Lucky for us Aidon had a grin that made women want to fall at his feet.

The receptionist went to a large conference room and gestured for us to go inside. "Have a seat and I will get the detective."

I gaped at my mate. "How in the hell did you manage that one? I thought for sure she was sending us away."

Aidoneus smirked at me then nipped my lips. "I am my father's son. It comes in handy at times."

Stella snorted. "So, the lore about being irresistible is true? That seems unfair. Not only are you a god, and you could have any man or woman with the crook of one finger, but you also have the ability to sway mundie minds to do your bidding? Geez, we don't stand a chance."

Aidon shrugged his shoulders. "I rarely use that power. In fact, I wouldn't have used it now unless it was absolutely necessary. As for my father, he's blamed for sins people commit when he has never even met them. Unfortunately for him, that rumor started after he encouraged a woman to castrate her cheating husband thousands of years ago when women were supposed to be meek little lambs that allowed their husbands to have sex with whomever they wanted without consequence."

One of my eyebrows lifted to my hairline, however the questions on the tip of my tongue died when a good-looking middle-aged man with café au lait skin and green eyes walked into the room and sat at the end of the table.

His forehead furrowed. "Gertrude told me you'd like to speak with me about a murder but didn't clarify. I have very little time at the moment, so I'll get to the point. Who are you guys are and how did you convinced her to let you back here when it isn't something she would do without a case reference?"

He caught me off guard and I pasted a smile on my face. "I'm sorry to interrupt your busy day, Detective Richardson, but we work for an online newspaper and need information on any odd murders that might have occurred in the area over the past few months."

The detective leaned forward with his arms on the table. "You can request information like every other member of the press. I don't have time to give out statements to every Tom, Dick, and Harry wanting information. You know there are proper channels that you must go through."

I cringed at the venom in his voice. I knew the lie I'd pulled out of left field was thin, but I also knew outright asking about weird deaths would raise more of his suspicions and get us nowhere. I knew press obtained information from police stations through official channels and I already had Selene working on that angle. I simply didn't think the police would release information that might indicate a supernatural victim or weapon. They'd want to keep that under wraps until they understood what was happening.

"Furthermore," the detective continued, "why are there

four of you here? Don't you guys work alone? Who are you really?"

My heart raced faster making me slightly dizzy. I'd lost track of the energy I'd picked up when we walked through the door to the rear of the station, so I opened my senses once again.

Aidoneus met the detective's gaze and held it. "We are a group of private investigators. We're here to gather as much information as possible for our open cases."

Detective Richardson rolled his eyes and stood up. "Look, I don't have time to give you information. If you're looking for missing persons information, you can submit your request through Gertrude. Be sure to include name, date of birth and all descriptive information you have available."

Aidoneus stood up with the detective. "You're going to stay and answer our questions."

Detective Richardson's forehead crumpled before he ran a hand over his short, black hair. He shook his head and opened his mouth. It was at that moment that I felt Aidon's energy pulse out of him like a slow heartbeat. It was subtle yet made me relax. I found myself wanting to answer him. I'd never felt that from him, and wouldn't have if I hadn't been probing the building for what I had sensed upon entering the heart of the station.

Richardson slumped into his seat. "What did you want to know again?"

Aidoneus looked at me and I shook my head. He had a hold of his mind, who knew if me asking would release him from that spell. It would be better if Aidoneus asked the detective what we needed to know.

Aidon inclined his head. "Have there been any odd murders in the area over the past six months or so?"

The detective laughed but the sound had no mirth. "Every murder is odd in some way. Well, except the domestic cases.

Those are usually straightforward. You're going to have to be more...wait, there was a case involving a young woman discovered on a hiking trail. It isn't my case, but we've all been involved because of the fur covering her arms. That was some weird shit."

A gasp escaped me as I sat forward. "What did the fur look like? Was she just hairy?"

Richardson's gaze shifted and he blinked several times as he stared at me. Crap, it seemed like Aidon's influence was wearing off. Another pulse of Aidoneus's magic and the detective's eyes took on a thousand-yard stare.

"It wasn't normal hair. It was black and there were spots in it like a panther. The doctors that tried to save her said they thought she got furrier and that her teeth changed to large canines while they were working on her. It was creepy as hell," Richardson explained.

Dread sat in my stomach like a boulder. "When was she found? Has her family claimed her yet?"

The detective shook his head from side to side. "About a week ago, I guess. Given the peculiarity of the victim, my Captain called in the FBI, so they took over the case. I haven't heard if her family has been found. I know the FBI is searching for them."

"How was she killed? Did they find a weapon?" Aidon interjected.

Richardson shook his head from side to side. "She'd been cut with what our ME said was an ax, but nothing was certain. There was very little evidence where she was found because she was killed somewhere else and dumped on the trail."

I suppressed the fear churning through me. This case had just gotten a lot more problematic. The mundane authorities had the body of a dead shifter and the freaking FBI was involved. "Where is the body located now? Is she still in North Carolina, or has she been moved somewhere else?"

Richardson tilted his head to the side. "She's still in the county morgue. The FBI just got involved. The local agent assigned to the case called in their forensics experts to examine her body. He had the ME collect samples from her in the meantime. They were supposed to be sent off today."

Tseki stood up so fast his chair hit the wall behind him. "We have to intercept those samples. The government can't get a hold of them."

The detective stood up, as well. Unfortunately, he seemed to come to his senses. "What do you want to keep from the government?"

Aidoneus joined the men, as did Stella and I. Aidon clapped Richardson on the shoulder. "We need to make sure one of our clients doesn't send compromising pictures of a prominent figure to those at the top. You know how burned spouses can be. Thank you for taking the time to talk to us. We'll get out of your hair. You won't even recall that we were here."

Detective Richardson scowled for a second before nodding. "You're welcome."

I practically ran from the office with Stella right beside me. Aidon and Tseki brought up the rear. We were a few steps outside when Stella started talking. "This is bad. We need to get that victim, and those samples, before anyone gets a hold of them. We also need to erase any evidence of her existence in the system."

I placed a hand on her shoulder. "You're right, we do. One thing at a time. Aidon and Tsekani can go to the ME's office and get the samples. We will catch an Uber and call Mohan."

Aidoneus pressed a kiss to my lips. "We will see you soon. Watch your back."

I nodded up at the man I loved. "Always do."

Tsekani chewed his lower lip. "I don't like leaving you like this, but it can't be helped. You two be careful. And tell Mohan we will take the victim if we can manage it, but it would still be wise if he called in his contacts to handle the removal of the body and all the evidence."

Stella held up her phone. "The car will be here in five minutes. We've got this. You don't have time. Go. Now."

The guys left and I pressed the paranormal police officer's contact in my phone. He answered on the third ring. I quickly brought him up to speed on the situation. "We aren't equipped to destroy all traces in the mundane system while also searching for the murderer. And honestly, that's my priority right now. This person has killed two in a short time span."

Mohan sighed into the phone. "I agree with you completely. Something dangerous is going on here and if you are willing to remain on the hunt for the perp, I will take care of the police system. That won't take as long and I can get back to the case I am on right now. Can you send me Tsekani's cell number so I can find out if they got the victim out of the ME's office? I can be there in a few hours, so I'm hoping they can get her out of mundie hands."

I tracked the grey SUV that just pulled into the parking lot. I could see the Uber light in the front window. I needed to wrap this up. "I'll send it as soon as we hang up. I will want to examine this victim, too, so if you are the one to retrieve her, please let me know."

Mohan agreed before he thanked me and hung up. It had been a long day and I was exhausted mentally. I considered taking a short nap when we got back to the rental house then discarded the idea. "What do you say we go get an apple martini instead of going to the rental? I know a place that has the best ones in North Carolina."

Stella brightened as the car pulled up to the curb next to

us. "That sounds much better than going back to wait until it's time to take Greyson to the mountain. I was already thinking about how we could do searches online to pass the time."

Laughing, I gave the driver the change of destination then texted Aidoneus to let him know where to meet us when he and Tseki were done at the ME's office. Guilt tried to push its way onto the main screen of my mind. But there was no way I was going to feel bad about relaxing for an hour or so before continuing with what I needed to do. I'd learned long ago that I needed to take care of myself. There was nothing wrong with getting a drink at the moment. The evidence was in the vehicle with Aidon and I had Selene researching what she could on the computer. It would be better in the long run for everyone involved if I shared a drink with my best friend.

CHAPTER 9

*S*ipping my second apple martini, I sighed and looked around the restaurant. "This is just what the doctor ordered."

Stella giggled. "We'd better get an appetizer or I will be more than tipsy by the time we head to the mountain."

I shook my head with a smile then lifted my hand to signal the waitress. "Good point. That meeting with the detective took longer than expected. They have the best stuffed mushrooms and bruschetta here."

"I see some things never change." The voice that said those things made my heart drop into my gut at the same time I fought the urge to throw a punch. Why the hell was this man here right now? I never wanted to see him again in my life.

Turning, I didn't bother hiding my disgust. "Hello, Miles. And look who's with you, Demon Spawn. How are things in Hell?"

Miles glared at me as did his girlfriend. She was worse than any demon I'd ever encountered. Her blonde hair and perky boobs were as fake as the apple flavoring in my drink.

"That was uncalled for, Phoebe. It was entirely your fault that we divorced. You can't blame us."

Stella sputtered, spitting the cocktail all over Miles. "That's the biggest load of bull I've ever heard."

Miles sneered at my best friend. "I see you've regressed to your childhood friends. Your behavior suddenly makes sense. You're trying to go back to your high school days."

My fists clenched tight in my lap. It took great effort to keep from lashing out at my ex-husband. Seeing his face brought back all of the anger and hurt he'd inflicted when he'd left me. Familiar insecurities made me run my hands down the front of the designer top Tseki had insisted I wear. God, I hated how Miles could still make me feel like a frumpy fat woman that nobody wanted.

My attention was snagged when I watched Aidoneus walk through the door. His attention was focused on me entirely. My ex didn't merit any more of my focus. A smile spread over my face as Aidon reached my side.

His facial expression morphed into a seductive smile just for me. Cupping my cheeks, he bent and kissed me passionately. Part of me was hooting with laughter imagining the look on Miles's face while the rest of me realized how childish that was.

"Sorry we're late, love. Who do we have here?" Aidoneus asked pointedly. He had his suspicions.

I introduced him to Miles and his girlfriend. Aidon arched one eyebrow. "Ah, this is the dumbest man alive, then."

Miles spluttered for several seconds. "I don't know what she's told you, but she only has herself to blame for our marriage failing. She let herself go and had no pride in how she looked. What are you doing here anyway? You finally dragged yourself off the couch to come and see your son?"

Aidoneus growled low in his throat and I placed a palm

over his chest. The power vibrating beneath Aidon's chest nearly burned me. My mate was barely holding back. His anger felt like a sharp lash in the air. It smelled like brimstone, as well. He was going to kill Miles.

I was just as pissed, but feeding into Miles would only make matters worse. "Have *you* visited your son lately?"

I cringed inwardly as I threw my son under the bus. I hadn't meant to draw my children into this. But I wasn't going to let Miles make me feel bad when he rarely saw Jean-Marc.

In typical Miles' fashion, he scanned the area then scowled. "Where's Nina? You couldn't even bring her to see her father?"

I rolled my eyes at him. "Nina's at home with my mom and Nana because she's in school right now. But her cell phone is in perfect working condition."

Miles sneered at me. "Convenient." He leaned closer and squinted while looking at me. "What, you couldn't find anyone as reliable as Charity to do your chin waxes? You can't afford to come all this way for your beard, you know. The child support is for the kids, not you."

My heart cracked as I subconsciously touched my chin feeling for those two stubborn hairs that had first made an appearance about a year and a half ago. I thought I'd plucked them that morning, but sure enough I felt one of them.

Aidoneus opened his mouth and shut it when I put up my hand. "I'm sorry to see your imagination hasn't improved any. It's sad that all you can think of as an insult is money and a few stubborn chin hairs. Before you go off topic again, I wanted to thank you for being a cheating bastard, having the Demon Spawn there fire me, then have me blacklisted. My life couldn't be better now."

MIles's chin dropped to his chest. "I know that's not true. You are an in-home nurse for an old woman. You went from being a highly skilled scrub nurse to a glorified ass wiper. That's humiliating."

Tsekani plucked the lapels of Miles's jacket. "What's embarrassing is how hard you're trying to be better than everyone else. This suit might be expensive but your body ruins the entire thing. And that hair." Tseki tisked at Miles. "You should give up trying to make it look fuller. You can't hide the fact that you're balding. I can't even say you have arm candy going for you because she's just...mediocre."

I tried to hold back the laugh that wanted to bubble up. Miles's face turned as red as an apple as the waitress came up to the table. Smiling at Miles, I ordered four different appetizers then handed her the black credit card for my business.

"I'll be letting my lawyer know you spend *my* money on yourself rather than the kids. The court will not be happy to hear you're galivanting around the world while your mom takes care of my daughter," Miles gritted through a clenched jaw.

Aidoneus was pressed against my side. "You're even crazier than I thought if you think you Phoebe is neglecting Nina. The love Phoebe has for both of her kids astounds me and makes me love her even more. But I'm not surprised a narcissistic asshole like you projects his bullshit onto his ex-wife. I imagine it must be hard to live with the knowledge that you ruined the best thing you've ever had."

Stella picked up a mushroom as the waiter delivered the platter. "And for the record, your ex-wife flew us here in her personal plane. Because she's everything you're not...intelligent, beautiful, and caring...she inherited a company worth more money than you can comprehend. And, no. You won't be able to take her back to court and take *her* money. The lawyers have already made sure of that."

Miles glared at me. "You can hide behind your lies and your friends, but know this. I will be taking you to court to get Nina away from you. The last thing she needs is to turn out like you."

Aidoneus stepped into Miles's face and I grabbed his arm. "Ignore him. Stella's right. The lawyers already know all about how he is and can deal with his bullshit."

I purposefully turned my back to my ex and pulled Aidoneus with me. It took several seconds before Aidon moved. I was convinced he was going to kill my ex. Relief swamped me as Aidon pressed kisses to the side of my neck.

Shaking off the interaction was tough to do, though. There was a second that I considered hexing the insufferable man. It was the thought of Nina and Jean-Marc that held me back. They loved their dad. Knowing that Miles didn't pay rent, so shouldn't be taking up space in my mind, I focused on my great friends and the love of my life. With a smile, Stella and I tasted each of the appetizers. Miles said something that I chose to ignore. I have no idea when he left because I magically shut him out.

Stella wrinkled her nose. "I can't believe you spent twenty years with that man. He puts all of his shit onto you. I would have slit his throat in his sleep if I'd been you."

I laughed as I ate another mushroom. "There were times I worried my kids would grow up without me for sure." I wiped my face and my hand moved over the chin hair.

Aidoneus must have noticed because he placed a kiss to my cheek. "Don't give it a second thought."

I sighed as I shook my head. "I need to give it more than a second thought because I hate these stubborn chin hairs."

Stella scowled at me. "Don't you dare let that man make you feel bad about yourself. He doesn't pay rent so he shouldn't be taking up space in your head."

I chuckled at my best friend. "Oh, it's not about him at all. My head is a far too busy place to be lowered to his level.

Besides, my mate is the sexiest man alive and makes Miles look like a toad in comparison."

Tseki gave me a fake frown. "I had no idea you hated toads so much."

We all burst out laughing as Aidoneus pulled a stool next to mine. He and Tsekani took a seat at the table and ordered a drink. "I really should apologize to frogs for that one."

"What we need to do is come up with a magical spell to get rid of the chin hairs. I spend more of my day plucking the three than I do brushing my hair. They always pop up like daisies even after I yank them out," Stella said, changing the subject.

God bless her. I loved that she knew precisely how to shift the mood back to fun and laughter. I refused to think about what an asshole Miles was. It was nothing new and not at all surprising. I was completely over him and what he'd done to me. He would reap the repercussions of his actions.

"I'm certain someone in the coven has already come up with something." We weren't the first women to deal with random facial hair popping up.

Aidoneus wrapped his arm around the back of my chair. "You're perfect as you are, Queenie. Don't change a thing."

I pressed a kiss to his lips. "I can't promise that. I hate the hairs and want them gone. And it has nothing to do with Miles. This is about me."

Tsekani smiled at the waitress when she checked on us and ordered an apple martini. "I'd have to kick your butt if you felt that way because of him. It's not as obvious as the asshat made it seem. Although, a magical spell would be a good idea."

Aidon groaned. "Promise me one thing, Queenie. Don't mess with magic you don't understand on your faces. You never know what could happen."

I looked at Stella for several seconds before we both

nodded at the same time and then laughed. "We won't do anything without thorough research. Back to more important matters. Did you guys manage to get the, uh, samples?"

Tseki lifted his drink. "The ME refused to cooperate until Aidon did his thing. The delay meant we had to track the shipping carrier down. Thankfully, the shifter's body was still in the building when I found her, but we couldn't get her out. There were too many mundies around."

I sighed and leaned into Aidoneus. "It's good to have the samples, but couldn't she just take more?"

"Don't worry though, we were able to hide her so Mohan's people could start erasing all traces of her in the system," Aidoneus explained in a low voice so those around us didn't overhear our conversation.

A weight lifted from my shoulders. "Where the hell did you hide her in a government facility so that Mohan can get to her?"

Tsekani shuddered and said a silent prayer. "We put her in the freezer with the unidentified bodies. They rarely go in there and with her being erased from their databases, they won't go looking for her."

I hated the thought of her being unidentified and forgotten. I sucked in a breath as a thought occurred to me. "Wait a minute. *They* won't have forgotten about her. What do we do about their memories? There is no way I'm asking Marius's people to help with their memories."

"We don't have to worry about that. It's one of the reasons I was glad Mahon agreed to handle that side of things," Tseki replied. "We have the longer, and harder, part of this case because he has the infrastructure already in place to handle this situation. He likely already has an entire team mobilized and working on everyone and everything they need to erase."

I nodded and drank the rest of my martini, then considered another one. I should have realized the paranormal police would have a system in place. Their primary directive is to ensure the existence of supernaturals remains a secret. If they weren't good at their jobs, the cat would have been out of the bag long ago.

"That's a relief. While we have no leads, I'd rather hunt down clues than deal with the rest of it. And it's almost time to meet the kids but I think there's time for one more. Oh, and Tseki, would you find someone to fix the damage in the kids' house while we are gone at the mountain? I don't want that being left to them. They have enough on their plates right now."

Tsekani lifted his glass signaling the waitress for another round. "I'm one step ahead of you and have already made some calls."

"I love that you know me so well," I replied.

Tseki placed a hand on my shoulder. "You have a big heart and I know how much you love those kids. I knew that would have been at the top of your mind if you didn't have so much on your plate. I'll always have your back, Phoebe."

Emotion burned at the back of my throat. "And I will have yours."

The waitress delivered our drinks and I didn't hesitate to suck mine back. I'd lost my pleasant buzz thanks to my slimy ex-husband and wanted to get it back. The night would be easier if I wasn't wound tighter than a grandfather clock.

CHAPTER 10

The kids' house was a buzz of activity when we arrived a short while later. Stella and I got out while Tseki and Aidon waited inside the vehicle for us. We walked up the path right as Skylar and Greyson came out of the house carrying burned pots to a dumpster parked in the driveway. Glancing back at the car, I gave Tseki a grateful smile.

Emmie rushed up to me and threw her arms around my waist. "Oh my gosh, auntie, you are the absolute best. I was so worried about how to fix the kitchen on top of making sure Greyson was okay." Skylar and Greyson were right behind her nodding their heads in agreement.

I squeezed Emmie's shoulders. "I haven't been in touch as much as I wanted to be because this magical world keeps throwing curve balls at me, but I am always here for you guys. If you ever need anything, or are worried or have questions, never hesitate to call me, even if you need money. I know you guys hesitate to bother your mom, because of all she's done for you guys. But I can, and will, help you without a problem."

Emmie nodded. "Thank you. I forget mom said you were now a witch, too. We've kept to ourselves since learning about our magic. It's a relief to have someone like mom not far away. It's terrifying at times."

Skylar leaned into my other side. "It's not easy being on our own. Although Emmie takes care of things like paying the bills and stuff, it's hard for me because I don't know how to help her."

Stella patted Skylar's shoulder. "Charts can help things run more smoothly. I'll help develop a chore chart before we go that includes someone buying groceries. And, if it's too much, Emmie, you can ask your mom to take over paying the bills. As a mother myself, I know she wouldn't mind helping."

Emmie scrunched her face as she let go of me and headed inside the house. "I can't burden her with that. We each work part-time to cover a portion of the bills. It's the least we can do."

Fiona had done a great job with her kids. They were thoughtful, observant and hard working. I prayed that I'd done as good a job with my children. Speaking of which, I was tempted to suggest Jean-Marc move in with the three of them. It would give me an excuse to help out with things and provide them with a support system.

My son was looking for a place to move off-campus next year and, given his magic, I hated the idea of him living in some apartment complex somewhere given his magic. He needed to be surrounded by people that understood.

There was no way I was going to mention it though. Emmie would agree regardless of how they felt. Instead, I focused on what I could ensure happened. "Jean-Marc and Emlyn will be here soon. Did you guys discuss anything more about forming a coven of your own and what that would mean for you guys?"

Skylar picked up her purse from their entrance table and

then turned to face me. "We met up on campus briefly. According to Em, if we do this, we will all get a boost in our power. It's like we will supercharge each other."

Emmie rolled her eyes. "There's only a small increase in actual power. The boost is mainly felt if we are in an emergency situation and we actively pull energy from the others in the coven. The biggest impact for us is that our powers will stabilize."

Lilith had explained how covens worked to me and why I couldn't refuse to remain in the one Hattie had formed long ago. Many of the members relied on that connection to the Pleiades and would suffer if I withdrew. As a collective, we were stronger together.

Leaving those thoughts aside for now, I poked my head into the kitchen. A crew of three guys were hard at work fixing what had been damaged. Knowing that was being taken care of, I shifted my focus to the more pressing matter at hand.

"Stabilizing each other will benefit all of you. Let's get going so we can meet Jean-Marc and Emlyn." I'd already programmed the directions into my phone that Jean-Marc had texted to me. They'd discovered the most powerful intersection about a half an hour drive from the house.

The kids gathered what they needed and we climbed into the rental car. Aidoneus was behind the wheel and smiled at me as I sat in the passenger's seat. I turned to the side so I could see the rear of the vehicle. The kids had climbed in with Skylar and Greyson taking the rear seats.

Greyson was drawn and looked tired already, but I didn't feel him probing my magic again. He did lay his head against the headrest and closed his eyes for the drive. His color was still better than earlier. A shiver traveled through me as I considered again how close he was to losing control.

"Do you know what we need to do to form this coven? I'd

like to do this now to make getting through finals easier for all of us," Emmie said.

Her words tugged my gaze from Greyson to her. "I have no idea what needs to be done. Let me ask my familiar."

"Tarja, are you there?"

"I'm here, Phoebe." My familiar's voice was scratchy, indicating she had been napping. *"How can I help you?"*

"How are you feeling? Is the pregnancy proceeding smoothly?"

"It is early yet, but the kits are developing as expected. Now, what can I do for you?"

"I was curious about how the kids would go about forming a coven."

"That is a wonderful development. They can join anytime, but the strongest bonds are formed on the full moon at midnight. First, they need to take a vow of loyalty that includes a promise to never use their magic to cause harm to another member of their group and a name they will go by. They will need candles and herbs to enhance their spell. It is best to do this outside, in a space they have cleansed. After the vow they need to develop bylaws or a code of ethics for their coven. Identifying a space for their gatherings isn't necessary to form the coven but is vital for them moving forward. After they take their vow, they are officially bound together."

"That seems simple enough. Thank you."

"Anytime. Are you heading to the ley line for Greyson now?"

"Yes, Aidoneus is parking the car as we speak. I will need your help tomorrow when I am hoping to get a look at the second victim we discovered."

"There was another killed in the same manner?"

Until that moment, I hadn't realized that I never told her about the shifter killed mid-change. I gave her a brief rundown of the visit to the police station and what we discovered.

"Take care when examining the shifter, Phoebe. If she was in a

partial shift, there is a chance that you will get a better feel for the magic. You might even be able to trace it. Let me know when you are with the body and I will join you."

"I will let you know as soon as I hear back from Mahon. Thanks again."

The car was silent when I ended the conversation with Tarja. Everyone was focused on me. I cleared my throat. "Sorry." I opened my door wanting to talk as we walked. "From what Tarja said it's fairly simple to form a coven. You should do it on the full moon at midnight to form the strongest bond possible and given that you are going to have two men join your group, I think that will be your best approach."

"I would agree," Emlyn added as she and Jean-Marc joined us.

I hugged my son in greeting. "My familiar said you guys pledge a vow to one another as you cast a spell binding you all together. Include a name for your group and make some bylaws. That's pretty much it."

Emlyn smiled as we walked down a path from the small parking area. "We will need a gathering place, which I am hoping can be your house. Neither Jean-Marc nor I have anywhere safe given that we live in the dorms."

Emmie nodded in agreement. "That will work. Let's talk about when we can do this, after we take care of the guys."

Skylar extended her hand in front of her as the path narrowed and sloped down sharply. The air was alive around us. It vibrated with energy that pulsed throughout the ground, trees, and shrubs, as well.

The energy made my blood fizz and bubble as it coursed throughout my body. We seemed to pass through a barrier. I paused for a second to wonder what its purpose was. It wasn't trying to keep us out.

When I saw the teal light glowing all around us, the answer hit me. The magic of the area must have a built-in protection that kept the mundies from discovering the power. If anyone other than a paranormal caught sight of the light surging up from the rocky ground beneath us, they would know something supernatural was occurring. That was the only explanation possible.

Being near the crossroads made me feel like I was Wonder Woman, capable of running around the center of the Earth. Energy poured into me at a rate that made me lightheaded.

The smell of the forest shifted from dirt and plants to that of a summer day after it had rained. We continued a few more feet until we reached a small clearing that was big enough for Jean-Marc and Greyson. The two of them stood in the center of the grassy field while we remained at the edges.

Aidoneus came up behind me and wrapped me in his arms. I leaned back into him and watched as my son spoke with Greyson. They'd grown up together and had always been close, like cousins.

"You need to draw the energy inside," Jean-Marc instructed.

Greyson closed his eyes and inhaled several times. A few seconds later, Greyson's skin seemed to glow like he was a light bright with bulbs beneath his skin. It was creepy as hell to see him like that. Imagine what it looked like when you held a flashlight behind your hand. It was like that only his entire body looked like that as electricity traveled over his skin arcing and snapping as it moved. It crackled in the silent night air. Glancing over at my son, I noticed he had the same blue lightning covering him, but he didn't look like a macabre light bright. His skin didn't glow enough that I could see the structures beneath like Greyson's.

Power hummed all around the two of them. Greyson started twitching and the power died suddenly. His eyes snapped open and widened when they landed on Jean-Marc. Greyson lifted his arm. "It's not working for me."

Jean-Marc smiled at him and clasped his hands. "It was working. You didn't let it in. Your internal shields must be strong to hold this much energy at bay. You need to let them down and invite the energy inside your body."

Greyson's forehead furrowed. "I thought I was already doing that. I repeated the chant that I wanted to take the power I felt flowing into me. Yet, the core of my power is still running on empty."

Jean-Marc shot me a look. There was a split second where I saw the panic in my son's face. It disappeared as fast as it popped up. Jean-Marc took a deep breath. "Tell me what it's like for you when you start getting low on magic."

Greyson scowled then turned away from my son and paced to the edge of the clearing where Aidon and I were standing. Greyson's lips were thinned and the tendons in the sides of his neck stood out.

He was clearly agitated as he turned and marched back toward Jean-Marc. No one spoke a word as Greyson paced. I thought he was going to remain silent until he stopped and finally broke his silence. "I've been terrified for weeks. My mom told me what happened when a witch or mage steals power from another. I clamped down on my magic when I felt it reaching for my sisters. My heart stopped when it wrapped around their power."

Greyson sobbed and shifted tear filled eyes to his sisters who were clinging to one another to the right of me. "I forced it back and built a brick building around the core of my power. I didn't realize it was starting to leak past that until you visited, auntie. I've been holding on by my fingernails and I'm damn tired."

Jean-Marc smiled at Greyson and clapped him on the back. "I can understand what you went through. I never got that close, but that fear rose despite that. And it is something that is easy to overcome. I want you to remove that brick house and let yourself go completely."

Greyson sucked in a breath. "I can't. It's going to try and take from my sisters. It wants their power, badly."

"That's not going to happen. Here it will soak up the readily available energy pulsing off the ley line," Jean-Marc told him.

Greyson looked at me and I nodded. "He's right. It's why we brought you here. But don't worry, I will protect them if you should make a grab for them."

Greyson nodded keeping his focus on me. "I'm trusting you to protect them."

"I will not let anything bad happen, you have my word," I promised.

Greyson closed his eyes and the glow was back beneath his skin. The electricity followed suit. Jean-Marc leaned closer to him. "Let down your walls. It's safe. Trust me, I would never allow you to harm anyone."

The glow dimmed beneath Greyson's skin while the blue lightning skipped across the surface. A smile bloomed across his lips and his eyes snapped open. "It's working."

Greyson laughed and threw out his hands. Power flowed into and around him for several seconds before stopping. Jean-Marc gave him a one-arm hug. "Now let's charge our lodestones. You brought yours, right?"

Greyson stuffed a hand in his front pocket and pulled out an iridescent rock. Holding it out on his hand, he nodded. "How do we charge this?"

"To charge your lodestone, you need to funnel the power you feel around you to the pulse in the center of the rock. You can cast a spell to make it easier. I found my intent was enough without spoken words. The energy wants to be absorbed and the stone was made specifically for that purpose, so it needs little prompting," Jean-Marc explained as he took his rock from his pocket.

"Sounds easy enough," Greyson replied.

I wasn't surprised when the stones started glowing as lightning covered the surface. It took seconds for that to finish. Once it was done, the guys headed back in our direction.

Jean-Marc and Greyson both had huge smiles on their faces. We followed them down the path as Greyson turned to face Jean-Marc. "I'd like you to come and live with us. I've already talked to Emmie and Skylar and they agree. I need the support and it will help if I have you to help remind me. I can't help how I instinctively fight against my sisters and I don't want to take a chance again."

My heart soared. This is precisely what I had hoped would happen. It lifted a huge load from my shoulders. I would worry less about all of them and it allowed me to help support all four kids.

Jean-Marc looked back at me. "I think it's a great idea. You all need to lean on each other throughout the next few years as you learn control. It's not as if you four are strangers. It's safer there than in an apartment by yourself. Before you say anything, I know you want to be on your own but right now is not the best time with the changes that you've gone through."

Greyson held his stone up in his palm and was moving the finger of his other hand around making the lightning follow its movement. "You don't want to have to clean an entire apartment by yourself, dude. Not to mention that we have a spare bedroom, so you'll have your own space."

I laughed as my son smiled in response. "I'd love to live in your house. The year ends soon, and I have to be out of the dorm in a month, but I can start moving stuff now."

My relief washed over me, making me giddy. It was so much easier knowing Jean-Marc and Greyson would have each other daily. Not to mention the additional support Emmie, Skylar and Emlyn would have.

Aidoneus brought my hand to his lips for a kiss, while the kids were talking excitedly about Jean-Marc moving in with Stella saying it would help the chore chart to have the four of them.

Jean-Marc lifted arms that still had remnants of electricity traveling over them as he turned to walk backward. "Now that Greyson is better, we should celebrate with pizza."

My laughter was cut off when I heard the slam of a car door. We were a few feet from the parking lot and I ran forward to see a black sedan pulling onto the road. My heart dropped to my feet when I caught sight of the specialized license plate as it sped away.

A curse left my lips when I recognized the license plate, HRTDCTR. "Your father just saw the magic traveling over your body. I think we're screwed."

Aidoneus cursed a blue streak as he raced for the edge of the lot. "Don't worry, Queenie. I'll erase his memory as soon as I get my hands on him."

Jean-Marc clenched his fists at his sides as magic sparked from him and hit the ground. Emlyn had backed away from him and I couldn't get close. He cast me eyes that told me he was resigned. "But can you erase his hatred and disgust? He despises anything out of the norm and won't like that his children now have magical powers. He'll see us as freaks."

I ignored the pain as I was stung by the lightning coming off him and wrapped my arms around my son, pressing a kiss to his cheek. "You aren't a freak. Try not to worry about your father right now. Aidon and I will handle him. Let's get that pizza."

"Thanks, mom. I love you," Jean-Marc replied.

"To the moon and back, sweetheart," I finished as I closed his car door once he was sitting in the driver's seat. I would move Heaven and Earth to make sure that asshole didn't expose my kids or make their lives any harder.

CHAPTER 11

*W*e were sitting in the kitchen/living room area of the kids' house. Jean-Marc was relaxed on the couch with Emlyn. Both looked like they felt right at home which was a good sign this new arrangement would work. I groaned as I shoved the last bite of garlicy crust into my mouth. We'd ordered pizza from the kid's favorite restaurant. They covered their crust in fresh garlic before cooking it so the flavor baked into the edges.

"What about Coven of the Night Garden for our name?" Skylar suggested around a bite of food.

Emlyn drained her Coke and got up to put the can in the recycling container. "I like that one. How do you feel about The Sacred Flame Coven?"

Jean-Marc stuffed the entire crust of one piece into his mouth. "I like them both." It was amazing that he was able to speak with so much in his mouth at the same time. It was incredibly gross to see the food rolling around behind his teeth.

Emmie pursed her lips and tilted her head to the side.

"Those are both good. I had thought of The Sacred Circle for us, but I like the Sacred Flame."

Greyson waved his pizza through the air as he spoke. "We should do a combination of the three names."

It was interesting that the girls had been considering what to call their coven while the guys hadn't given it a second thought. The difference in the ways of thinking between the sexes couldn't have been more obvious.

"What about the Sacred Garden Flame?" Stella's suggestion incorporated most of that they'd suggested. "You guys are one of the only covens to have their own pixie caring for their garden. Which reminds me. You guys will want to start an herb garden. She can take care of it. But don't you dare take her for granted."

Emmie and Skylar looked at each other, then included Emlyn who nodded her head. Emmie smiled. "That's perfect. We have our name and most of what we need for the ritual."

Skylar picked up her phone and tapped an app. "The full moon is in three nights. We will have time to get what we need before then. I never thought about making our own herb garden. I know mom mentioned it, but it seems like a ton of work."

I glanced around the area, noting the door at the opposite end of the room and the French doors to our right that lead to the backyard. Getting up, I opened the side door and glanced outside. "There's enough room over here for a small greenhouse. I'll have one built there so you can access it from inside the house. That way you will have fresh herbs year-round. I'm told those are better for your work."

"They're much better for potions and tinctures," Emlyn pointed out. "My mom only uses fresh ingredients. I thought I'd have to wait until I was done with college and had a home of my own before I would have access to them."

Emmie and Skylar started asking Emlyn questions while

Greyson and Jean-Marc moved to the television and turned on a video game. I leaned my head against Aidoneus's chest and watched for several minutes.

"We should probably go find the asshat and make sure he doesn't blab what he saw." I hated to break into the serenity of the moment but I knew Miles was likely chomping at the bit if he hadn't already gone to the police.

Aidon shook his head from side to side making his jaw brush against my head. "There's no need. I'll take care of him after I get you and Stella to the house to rest. He's a mundie and not likely to tell anyone what he saw. Stop and think about it. If he'd come home years ago and told you he saw lightning sparking from your son's body, what would you say to him?"

I sat up and turned to face him. "I'd ask him if he felt alright then check his schedule. Doctors often have surgeries that last more than fifteen hours making them more than a little loopy."

Jean-Marc turned halfway around and waved his game controller at us. "I can call dad and ask for his help on a project for biology class. I was going to do one on the circulatory system since I have more knowledge than most already and it will feed dad's ego in the process. I'll know right away if he suspects anything."

I wanted to tell Jean-Marc no, absolutely not. "If you will call him the day after tomorrow, that would be best. He's too smart to dismiss the event as a trick of light and he might be dumb enough to say something to someone despite how it will make him look. I want Aidon to have time to pay him a visit if necessary so he doesn't say something to you he will regret and that will ruin your relationship."

Jean-Marc made a face. "You're doing it again, mom. You don't always have to try and make him look better to us. Or cover for him. It's not your job and never was. I know he's my dad but he's not a nice guy. I don't know how you put up with his crap. I hope I'm never an ass like him."

My heart skipped a beat. I had made excuses for Miles so long it was second nature at that point. Even then, I had to clamp my mouth shut to keep from telling my son his father wasn't an ass. He was much worse than that and I was glad my son saw it. It meant there was hope for him.

"You will never be like your father. You're sensitive, thoughtful, and caring and you always have been."

Jean-Marc smiled at me before returning to his game. Aidoneus cupped my cheek, gazing at me with eyes full of love and affection. Having someone that loved me that much made my heart fuller than I imagined possible.

Aidon pressed his lips to mine briefly. "You astonish me more every day. I don't understand how you lived with that man for two decades, Queenie. His aura smothers anything in its orbit. I cannot imagine even an ounce of your brilliant light being dimmed by him."

I refused to think about how it was during my marriage. Instead, I focused on the love I had for Aidoneus. "We can drive by on our way to the rental house if that's alright. Right now, I'd rather focus on finding the killer attacking paranormals. Specifically, how I might go about finding the person that called me or the killer himself. I have wondered if perhaps Marius might have put these murders in motion before I killed him."

Aidon wrapped his hands around my mine. "It's entirely possible. Unfortunately, we can't ask him now. Assuming he is behind them, what does that tell us?"

I couldn't help the pang that shot through me when I was reminded that he was no longer around to be questioned. My guilt was irrational, but there nonetheless. "It tells us the caller is connected to the vampires. The time of day we received the call rules out that person being one of the undead."

Stella cocked her head to the side as she looked up from the chart she was making for the kids. "Oh, it could be a thrall of his. Perhaps after you killed him, they came to their senses."

I considered Stella's theory. "If that was the case then where are they right now? I don't think the caller and the killer are the same person. Nina said the caller was terrified."

Aidon's forehead furrowed as he looked at me. "The thrall angle doesn't feel right. I agree with Phoebe that once that was broken, most people would have done something. I can see a mundie going to the police to report they were forced to bait someone in connection to a murder. Mundies don't have experience with death."

"I would freak the hell out then go to the police before I worried about why I did what the guy asked. I'd be afraid the person would come after me and would want protection," Stella admitted.

That described at least ninety percent of the mundie population. Even those accustomed to taking lives would be freaked out by blindly doing what some stranger asked them to do. That manipulation coupled with murder was enough to rule out mundies in my mind.

"Alright, so the caller wasn't a mundie which tells me it is unlikely Marius was behind these murders."

Tsekani lifted a hand. "Not to mention vampires would drain the victims of their blood before cutting them up."

Emmie and Skylar gasped then went pale. I got up and moved to the table where they were sitting with Emlyn. "Sorry, they forget not everyone sits around having graphic discussions. We will save that for later, but I want you girls to be extra careful when you're going to and from classes and work. Someone is killing supernaturals in the area which means you are in danger."

Emmie set her Coke can down with a shaking hand. "I'm so glad you're here looking into things. It makes me feel safer."

Aidoneus stood up and joined me. "I have already called some of my agents and asked that they come keep an eye on you guys. It's a good idea if you all stay here for the time being and leave in pairs. My men will be wearing all black with red shoes, so you will know they're friendly and not stalking you."

"When did you arrange that?" I never heard him call Thanos or anyone else about the issue.

Tseki chuckled. "When I called the contractors on the way home. He mentioned his concern for their safety with a killer on the loose."

I wrapped an arm around his waist. "We make a great team, Yahweh."

Jean-Marc groaned. "Don't get mushy in front of us, mom. I'm already losing this game and can't afford the distraction."

I winked at my son before ruffling his hair. "On that note, we're going to get out of here. You guys listen to Aidon and stay together. I'll call to check in tomorrow." I wanted to get out of there and stop by my old house and my eyes were starting to gloss over. My stamina had increased with all our adventures, but I still had a point where my body would stop cooperating.

"Love you mom," Jean-Marc said without getting up.

Greyson forgot the game, got up and wrapped his arms around me. "Thanks for not letting my anger scare you away and insisting I get my shit under control. You and Jean-Marc saved our lives."

"I'm only a phone call away. Call me if you need anything," I told Fiona's son.

The girls gave me hugs and said their goodbyes. Stella clapped me on the back as we walked out to the car. "Are we headed to the asshole's house now?"

"Yes, I want to make sure he isn't planning something nefarious." I glanced at Aidoneus and noticed the way he flinched.

Aidon opened my car door and pulled me into a harsh kiss before I could climb inside. His fingers wrapped in my hair and tugged my head back as he plundered my mouth. The fingers of his free hand pressed deeply into the small of my back, forcing my body against his.

His possession made my body heat with desire and my heart melt for him. He was staking his claim on me in a way no one ever had. Not even him. I surprised myself when I realized that I loved it.

"What was that for?" My lips were numb and I was sucking in air like a dying man, so I wasn't sure I spoke actual words.

"I've been wanting to do that for hours." He nudged me into the vehicle then closed the door as soon as my butt hit the leather.

He was in the driver's side and pulling away before I gathered my wits about me. Stella's head appeared between the seats with a smile. "What do we do if he has already called the police?"

I turned so I was facing Aidon while looking back at Stella and Tsekani. "He's not likely to call the cops. It's far more likely that he'll have the head of the Psychiatric department over for a chat. They're long-time friends and golf buddies. Doctor Burke is probably the only one he could convince to put a hold on Jean-Marc or me without looking insane."

Aidoneus sped down the road and cut off a line of cars as he jumped on the freeway. "If they are there plotting and planning, I will unleash my full power on them."

That was interesting. I wondered how much power he'd used on the detective. "You haven't been using all of your abilities?"

Aidon shook his head from side to side. "I'd melt a human's brain, killing them if I let it all out. It might even kill supernaturals. Much like Greyson, I have lived with a lid on my powers for longer than I can recall." He pulled off the highway, following directions he must have memorized because I wasn't telling him where to go, yet he was heading in the right direction.

I smiled at him and took the hand closest in mine. "I can't imagine how that must be for you. I wish that wasn't neces- sary and am grateful that you have controlled what you unleash to save lives." He didn't have to be so careful with his power. He owed no one anything. That he did, showed what kind of a man, er god, he really was.

Aidoneus glanced over at me as he turned down the street that led to my old house. "Are you sure you want to drive by and see him?"

I was uneasy leaving as it was. There was too much at stake. "We have to make sure he isn't telling his Demon Spawn girlfriend about what he saw. I can't have Jean-Marc being berated by his father. He won't wait to get the all clear from me, he'll be thinking he can help protect me."

"I don't like it," Aidon insisted.

Realizing he might be insecure about me seeing Miles now that he knew about our magic, I grabbed his hand in mine. "I hope you know I only want to do this to protect my kids and the magical world. Miles is an asshole that will not hesitate to sacrifice his son if he thinks he can punish me. I have to make sure he doesn't turn this around and try to have

Jean-Marc committed. He's got enough influence at the hospital to warrant a psychiatric hold on him."

Aidoneus's eyes narrowed as he sucked in a breath then clenched his jaw. "He would never do that to his own child."

I snorted. "Miles is a selfish jackass. He only cares about himself, so yes, he would. He will use this knowledge somehow. I just don't know how yet. I need to make sure it doesn't backfire on Jean-Marc."

Aidoneus parked a few houses down and looked out the front window. Stella stuck her head between the seats. "That's where you lived with Miles? That house is almost as big as Hattie's."

I chuckled and shook my head. "Nimaha is almost three times bigger than this place. Yet feels far more cozy to me than this house ever did."

I held up my hand when we climbed out of the vehicle. "I'm going to cast an invisibility spell over us, so Miles can't see us checking on him."

Stella bounced on her toes. "I'll do a silencing spell so we don't have to worry about being overheard."

I gave my best friend a one-armed hug. "Let's do them both together. On the count of three." I took a deep breath and focused on making our movements silent and invisible. "One, two, three."

Stella nodded to me and together we said, "*tacet et invisibilia.*"

We walked down the street and I pointed to the car parked in the driveway. "Looks like his little tart is here with him. If she's his partner, he will likely tell her his plan."

Aidoneus stopped next to the black sedan Miles was driving and touched the hood. "He hasn't been home long. It hasn't cooled in the slightest. I wonder what he's been doing for the last two hours."

Stella made a sound of disgust. "Looks like he's in the

bedroom. We can encourage the tree in the backyard to carry us up to the balcony so we can listen to what he's telling his girlfriend."

I sighed and snuck through the gate leading into the backyard. I closed my eyes and pictured the root of the large oak tree growing and rising into the air until it reached the balcony.

"*Crescere et ortum,*" I chanted.

The ground rumbled and I shot a panicked glance to the bedroom window. When the root started growing and rising, I grabbed Stella's hand. "C'mon we need to get on this thing and get up there."

Aidon joined us but Tsekani stayed below and scanned our surroundings. I was so damn glad he was there ensuring we were safe. My mind was completely consumed by Miles and my fear over what he might say and/or do to Jean-Marc.

I wobbled, almost taking Stella over the side with me but Aidon steadied us. "Careful, Queenie. You might not want to look down."

I nodded, not wanting to tell him I'd been thinking about how I wasn't paying attention to my surroundings because of Miles. When the root stopped, we were right outside the window. I ducked down instinctively despite the invisibility spell.

To my surprise, nothing had changed inside the room. My jaw dropped when I saw the tart glaring at Miles with her hands on her hips. "Where the hell have you been? Did you go see your ex-wife? Did you have sex with her? I know she wants you back. I could see her jealousy when she looked at us together."

"Ugh, God no! It was a miracle I didn't throw up when I saw the vile man," I blurted.

Stella chuckled. "That woman is freaking delusional. She

might even need medication. Perhaps they can both go tell the cops and be hauled away because they're loco."

Miles held up his hands and wobbled. "I tried to see my son. That witch is poisoning him against me."

"And now we know what he was doing after he left the mountains. He's drunk as hell," I said seconds before his girlfriend accused him of the same thing.

"You want Phoebe back because you found out how rich she is now, don't you? You just don't know how to break the news to me. Is this because I broke up with you over the holidays? I already explained to you that I made a mistake when I did that," the tart went on to say.

Miles closed the distance between them and wrapped his arms around her. "I had to get drunk to wipe her ugly face from my mind. You're the only woman for me. And she might be rich right now, but I will sue her for every penny she has then we will be the rich ones."

"Don't worry," Miles's tart promised him. "I have a way to make sure she never bothers us again."

I heard Aidoneus growl behind me as bile filled the back of my throat. Miles simply made me sick to my stomach. It only got worse when he took her shirt off and she pushed his pants and underwear to his knees as he kissed his way down her neck to her pert boobs.

"*Defluxio,*" I muttered while battling nausea. Next, I cast the spell to make the root return to its normal size.

I held onto Aidon as the root lowered us to the ground. I bent over and hurled in the grass the second my foot touched it. I wiped my mouth with the back of my hand when I was done and stood up straight.

"Who else needs bleach for their eyes? God, I can't stand that man. He will never get a dime from me." I wasn't entirely surprised Miles wanted to take my money. He was a greedy slimeball.

Aidon ran a hand along my back. "I'll make sure he never hurts you again." He didn't need to tell me he wanted to kill my ex. It was written all over his face.

"I don't want you using any of your energy on him, Yahweh." I didn't want Aidoneus anywhere near Miles. Not because I wanted him to live but because I had no desire for my mate to be responsible for killing Miles. The kids liked Aidon and I didn't want to risk ruining their relationship.

Stella laughed and clapped Aidon on the shoulder. "Besides, I think Phoebe cursed him with explosive diarrhea. His night is about to get even worse."

I thought that would make Aidon laugh but it didn't. I ran a hand over his chest. "I figure that it's partial payment for threatening me like that. I am fighting back in the only safe way I can. But seriously, Yahweh, he doesn't deserve your energy. The lawyers already have protections in place so he will not have a leg to stand on. Let him spend his money and spin his wheels. We can decide if his memory needs to be adjusted after Jean-Marc calls him."

"You deserve to have your hundred and seventy-five pounds of flesh, Queenie. However, I like the way you think. With your power that spell is likely to keep him on the toilet for a few days." There was humor in Aidon's voice as he twined his fingers with mine.

We left the backyard that I'd poured so much of myself into and got back into the car. It had been a long freaking day and I was exhausted. All I wanted to do was take a hot shower and get some sleep.

CHAPTER 12

*A*idoneus's magical fingers rubbed my shoulders as we stood in the living room of the rental house. The house was similar to the one I'd lived in with Miles, which added to the feelings that bombarded me from the moment we had landed in North Carolina.

The strength and fortitude I'd gained over the past several months seemed to have vanished. But that wasn't entirely accurate. It was there under the insecurity and doubt Miles had always made me feel.

Aidoneus pressed his lips to my temple. "I can feel your brain working overtime, Queenie. I know better than to tell you to forget about that asshole, so let's focus on the killer we're here hunting. Have you heard from Mahon about seeing the shifter? I didn't have much time with her body, but I did sense something coming from her where I didn't with the elf."

That sounded promising. And it made me feel better about taking the time to meet up with Mahon to view the shifter victim. "I have an appointment with Mahon in the morning. That's our only lead at the moment."

Tsekani thrust his hands on his hips. "Phoebe Dieudonne`, stop that defeatist attitude right now. Between the evidence you can use to scry, the shifter, and my message on Facebook we will find a new lead."

My head snapped in Tseki's direction. "What are you talking about? Why would you leave a message on Facebook?"

"There's a private group on the platform for members of the magical world. Being the brilliant, best-dressed member of our team, I put a message up there asking for the anonymous caller to contact us again so we can get more information from them."

I smiled at him. "Have I told you how fabulous you are lately?"

Tseki cocked one hip and smirked. "Not in the last six hours. That should have brightened your mood. What's wrong? Is it that worm that treated you worse than a bug?"

Aidoneus stiffened next to me. It was difficult to ignore, but I wanted my friends to understand. "Miles has always had a way of making me feel like shit. However, it's not him per se. I'm used to him talking down to me and being a jerk. His comments didn't affect me much. It's the reminder of who I used to be when I was married to him."

Stella picked up the wine bottle from the table to fill my empty glass. "You have no reason to be ashamed of that time in your life, Pheebs."

I snorted, wishing she was right about that. "Don't I? How could I let him force me to do over ninety percent of the work raising the kids, including the household chores? And when I didn't have dinner prepared on time or the laundry done, I was a crappy mother who couldn't plan for shit. Never mind that I worked fourteen-hour shifts. I was a second-class citizen in my marriage, not a partner."

Aidoneus cupped my cheeks and looked into my eyes.

The rage coming off him nearly knocked me over. "I have no idea how you did all of that and lived with the guy. Not to mention that your kids are wonderful. That alone tells me he didn't spend much time with them. I can't pretend to understand how it must feel to have been in your shoes. I know that you know this, but you are none of those things he said."

I smiled as I went to my tiptoes and pressed my lips to his. "Thank you for always coming with me when I have somewhere to go. And for believing in me. I never had those things before."

Aidoneus didn't soften for a second

"It's clear he never considered your feelings or opinions either," Stella pointed out. "Diarrhea wasn't a strong enough hex for him."

Tsekani chuckled and rubbed his hands together. "We need to come up with something that might teach him a lesson. Given his focus on money, we should hex him to go broke."

Stella laughed. "Jerk face deserves a dose of his own medicine. We should get him, and his tart, fired from the hospital for robbing Phoebe of everything she worked for at that place."

Aidoneus growled. "I'm going to kill that asshole."

I ran my hands up and down his chest. "I'd rather you use that energy on loving me. I'm not his doormat anymore and I never will be again. Miles will get his own. I'm a firm believer in fate. After all, if I hadn't gone through all of that I would never have crossed paths with you, Yahweh."

Aidoneus picked me up faster than I could blink. My legs wrapped around his hips, bringing my core in contact with his growing erection. Tseki and Stella whistled and whooped, saying something about getting some. I didn't hear them as Aidon was carrying me down the hall.

My arousal started slow given the day we'd had. But

thanks to the friction between our groins, it was gaining momentum like a racehorse shooting out of the gate with every step he took.

"I love you, Yahweh. I would gladly go through every second of unhappiness I've ever lived to be here with you right now."

Aidoneus pressed his lips to my mouth and kissed the life out of me. At some point, he kicked the door shut behind us then pressed me against the wall just inside the room. He broke away, allowing me to breathe again, as he continued kissing his way down my neck and across my shoulder.

The space was dark, making it difficult for me to see anything. My fingers wound into his hair and my hips took on a life of their own, moving against his hard shaft. My ability to think fled as my heart raced.

It was impossible to reach behind me and take off my top. Aidon didn't let that stop him as his mouth went to my nipple and sucked it in along with my shirt and bra. It suddenly didn't matter than he wasn't licking my flesh. His talented tongue flicked the hard pebble making me groan.

I clutched the short strands of his hair, pulling him closer to my body. He chuckled and released my breast. Teasing me, he looked up through thick lashes with a smile. My heart stopped in that second as I gazed into his dreamy sapphire blue eyes.

The moment was perfect. I'd never felt more in one moment than I did right then. The love and affection in his depths took my breath away. I had no words to describe the effect it had on me. If I hadn't fallen for him before then, I would have been lost after that.

I'd waited several months to take our relationship to the physical level. Aidoneus was a god that had lived literally for thousands of years and had been with just as many women. I had no doubt there were likely men in there, too.

The idea intimidated the hell out of me, especially since the only guy I'd ever been with criticized everything I did in bed, as well. I wasn't intimate enough or I was too clingy. I didn't give him a blow job often enough. He wanted more skin until he got it and then would say I let myself go after the babies.

Needless to say, I had a complex to overcome before I could allow Aidon to even see me naked. And that wasn't even including the thought of how many previous partners he'd likely had raced through my mind like a rabbit through a forest.

Fortunately, Aidoneus's love for me erased every thought that wasn't about how good it felt to be with him. At that point our sex life took off faster than a Formula One car and I've never looked back.

I dropped my legs, needing to be naked with him now. He liked to tease me to the point of begging which was something I rarely had any patience for. Aidoneus lowered me to the ground. "Someone's anxious to move things along."

I growled at him. "Blame that talented mouth of yours. I know I do."

Aidon laughed as I kicked off my shoes, then pulled my shirt over my head. The top few buttons had already come undone, so that made it easier. Aidoneus backed up and watched as I unbuttoned my pants and pushed them to my knees. Lifting my hands above my head, I shimmied my hips making the fabric pool at my feet.

A groan slipped from my mate as he ran a hand over his mouth. In nothing but my panties and bra I made a god drool. That right there made me feel like the sexiest woman alive.

My brain short circuited when Aidoneus grabbed the back of his Henley and yanked it over his head. The muscles of his abdomen rippled as he tossed the fabric to the side. His sapphire eyes were lit with desire. "Would you like a bath? It's been a long day."

I shook my head from side to side as I unhooked my bra and let it fall to the floor. The hunger in Aidon's eyes made me forget I had any stretch marks on my boobs. It was amazing what the love of a good man could do for a woman's self-esteem.

"I'd rather you take me hard and fast first. We can shower after."

Aidon's eyes started glowing as if they were backlit. I meant to ask him about that. It didn't happen often which made me wonder if it was a sign some of his power was leaking past the control he had on it. "You make it difficult not to become a ravening beast."

I reached him and ran my hand up his bare chest. "I see you missed the memo. I like your beast."

Aidon's mouth hovered a few millimeters from mine. "I might hurt you, Queenie. I need to be careful."

I lifted to my toes then pressed my lips to his, pouring every ounce of desire into the kiss. Without breaking contact, I pushed my panties down my hips and reached for his fly.

Moving my mouth to the side of his, I murmured, "Even if you wanted to, you could never hurt me."

The sound of his zipper competed with our panting breaths. It was a sound that made heat course through me like lava through a volcano. It was a great example of a Pavlovian response. It was my cue to get lost in Aidoneus's arms.

His hard cock slid through my wet folds when he lifted me in his arms. His mouth moved across my collarbone while I squirmed, trying to rub myself against him. It was trapped between us now and he held me tight enough I couldn't get any friction.

Turning, he laid me on the bed, making me lose contact with his shaft. Before I could lift a hand to reach for him, Aidon was on top of me. He grabbed both of my hands in one of his as he slid his cock from my opening to my clitoris.

My hips moved, rubbing the delicate bundle of nerves. My eyes remained glued to his as he pressed down, making the contact harder. My arousal spiked and my body leaped to the edge of the cliff in one bound.

Aidon bit down on my neck as he slipped his free hand between us. After licking the mark his teeth left, his mouth moved to one breast while one of his fingers dipped inside me. My back arched, and a cry left my lips.

A second finger joined the first at the same time he sucked my nipple inside his mouth. I went up in flame, like the dryest kindling. The climax exploded out of me making me see stars. The sapphire glow of his eyes never left mine making the experience far more intimate.

He continued fingering me for several seconds while I came down. "You're gorgeous when you come apart, Queenie."

Aidon withdrew his touch, leaving his cock playing through my slit. I was sensitive for a few seconds before he had me right back on that edge, wanting more. He lifted his body up so I had very little pressure where I wanted.

My hands ran up his sides. One moved across his chest so I could tease his nipple while the other moved lower. I wasn't expecting his reaction when I grabbed his balls. He growled as he pulled his hips back then thrust into me all the way to the hilt. He didn't pause as he set a hard and fast rhythm. I moaned as I lifted my head to his for a kiss. He obliged by taking my mouth like he was my body. I was powerless beneath him and I loved it.

My hips swiveled making him hit all the right spots at once. My fists went to the bed beneath me and twisted in the sheets. It wasn't enough. I had to hold on as he gave me what I asked for, so I grabbed his perfect ass.

This man did things to me no man ever had. One of them was the way his love enveloped me along with his power. It was like another erotic caress when it touched mine. Our movements increased as I chased my climax.

He took care of me like he always did and pinched my clit. His name left my lips on a hoarse shout. He wrapped one arm around me and held me tight. A second later his hips stilled and his orgasm barreled from him.

We writhed in each other's arms as I pressed my forehead to his. "I love you, Yahweh."

"I love you too, Queenie. Forever and always."

Being in Aidoneus's arms, knowing how much he loved me, made the last of my insecurities melt away. The little imperfections didn't matter one bit. What mattered was what was in my heart and soul. My eyes slipped closed on that soothing thought.

CHAPTER 13

I stretched on the uncomfortable bed, groaning until I smelled the delicious smell of coffee coming from downstairs. The bed dipped beside me as Aidoneus rolled over and draped an arm over my torso. "You were restless last night, Queenie. Is it being where your old life used to be?"

Lifting his hand, I placed a kiss to his palm then sat up. "God, no. It's this freaking bed. This thing was like sleeping on a rock. I'm spoiled with the luxurious mattress I have at home."

Aidon bounced up and grabbed a t-shirt, covering his bare chest. "You didn't seem to mind the bed while I was making love to you."

I got up and hunted for a change of clothes in my suit-case. "Luckily for me you're good at making me lose my mind to our passion. We need to see if the other beds are more comfortable. I can't sleep in this again."

Aidon wrapped his arms around me from behind. "You can sleep on me if it comes to that. Coffee will help and it seems that either Tseki or Stella is already up and cooking breakfast."

I smiled up at Aidon. "The smell lured me out of bed. And as wonderful as that scent is, I'm going to need an energy drink at some point today if I hope to get through everything."

I shoved my legs into the only pair of nice slacks I had brought on this trip. They were a pair of designer ones that Tseki had insisted I needed for board meetings. I wasn't about to be caught by Miles or his tart looking less than fabulous. I might even have to send Tseki shopping for some more upscale clothes.

Aidoneus twined his hand with mine as we walked downstairs. Tseki was standing at the stove with a spatula in hand while wearing a purple apron with ruffles over his dress shirt and pants.

Stella sat at the island a couple of feet away. "Good morning. Are you ready to do this today? I've had some thoughts about what to do after we meet Mahon."

I held up a hand staving off further comment. "Caffeine first."

Tseki handed me a cup with a bow. "Here you are mi' lady."

I chuckled and stole a piece of bacon from the plate next to the frying pan. "Thank you, good sir. Were your beds like rocks, as well?"

"Mine was fine," Stella replied eyeing me as I sipped my coffee.

"Go ahead. What is your idea?" I waved her on with my free hand while drinking my java as fast as was safely possible.

Stella bounced as she turned to face me. "I was thinking we need to tap into the often-overlooked resources in the area. Namely the pixies that I saw hovering in the trees at the park where Jean-Marc usually goes to recharge his magic. They see everything. Most rarely think about them and what they might know. It's possible there were some where the victim was found."

Tseki brought a plate of eggs and bacon to the island. "And if they didn't see anything, they might have heard something that can help us. We can ask Mythia to use her influence, if necessary, but your reputation precedes you, Phoebe."

Stella grabbed a piece of bacon and held it up. "And not just because you handed Marius and his people their asses. Most paranormals love you as much as they did Hattie."

Emotion burned in my chest as I considered the honor. I was nowhere near as talented or proficient as Hattie, so to be regarded as highly touched me. Aidon kissed the top of my head as he stood next to me at the island. "I didn't know Hattie well, but I'm not surprised, Queenie. I've told you many times that you're nothing this world has ever seen before."

Aidon's belief in me bolstered my courage and had given me the strength to do most of what I had in the past eight months. Squeezing his hand, I considered Stella's suggestion. "You are brilliant, as well, Stella. You're right about the pixies being overlooked. I hadn't considered what they might have seen or heard. We will head there as soon as we finish with Mahon. Tseki, I need you to do something for me while we are gathering information."

One of Tseki's perfectly plucked eyebrows rose to his hairline. "And what might that be?"

I waved a hand at my chest. "I need you to pick me up some clothes that aren't jeans and sweaters."

Tsekani's mouth went slack before he snapped it closed with a smile. "You don't want that jerk and his skank to see you dressed down."

Behind me Aidoneus stiffened. I closed my hand around his, hoping to make him understand. "No, I don't. It's stupid and irrational. He doesn't matter at all. I rarely think about the man and am completely over him. Not to mention, I know there's a good chance I will ruin what you buy. Yet, for some reason I want them both to eat crow when they see me. I'm still working on self-doubt that Miles exploited and made worse. This will help."

I titled my head back to regard Aidon. "I love you with everything I am, something I never felt for Miles. I need you to know this has nothing to do with me wanting him, or me trying to make him jealous."

Aidoneus smiled serenely at me. "I think I understand. You're using their idea of what successful people wear as armor against them."

I jerked away as if he'd just stabbed me. Oh my, God. I was dressing for Miles. Like I had throughout our marriage. Designer clothes didn't make me happy, or mean I had money. My situation didn't change no matter what I wore. I promised myself I was always going to be comfortable.

Standing on tiptoes, I kissed his lips. "Thanks, Yahweh. That's just what I needed to hear. Never mind, Tsekani I have plenty of clothes with me."

Tseki made a noise of disgust. "I could still go grab a few things for you. I saw the perfect pair of Gucci jeans that would look good on you."

"And you could add a few nicer pieces in size eight, just to be sure," Stella added giving Tseki her size.

I rolled my eyes at them and grabbed a blanket from the back of the couch. "Shop to your heart's content, Tseki. You aren't needed for this part, anyway. We can meet up at the park. We'll bring lunch. That will be the best excuse to be hanging around there anyway. I'm going to change, then I'll be ready to go."

Stella leaned toward Tseki as I walked out. I heard her tell him about a navy pin-striped suit and pink silk shirt that she'd seen a few weeks ago. Laughing, I hurried up the stairs, I tore my top over my head, kicked off the heels and shoved the pants off. Grabbing the soft sweater that Nina gave me for my birthday, I tugged it on then added my favorite jeans and shoved my feet into my soft leather boots.

I sighed as I once again descended the stairs. The others were in the entryway waiting for me. Aidon smiled, gazing at me as if I was wearing a ball gown. "Your feet feel better already, don't they?"

I smirked and lifted a shoulder. "So much better. These boots have served me well and are so soft I hardly feel like I'm wearing them."

"I'll see you at the park. The Uber will be picking me up soon," Tseki said as we left through the front door.

"Sounds good. Let me know if you hear anything back on that Facebook message," I called back to him.

The dragon shifter nodded then closed the door. I programmed the address where Mahon had the shifter victim into the map app for Aidon to follow. I twisted in the seat to glance back at Stella. "Do you think we should call Kason? Our victim wasn't a wolf, but she was a shifter."

Stella turned her gaze from the window with pursed lips. "Honestly, I'm not certain. My gut says no, that his wolves stay in the pack, while many feline shifters live solitary existences. However, we're dealing with supernatural beings, so what do I know?"

"You're right that most felines are solitary, but shifters are different. They tend to stick together, just in smaller packs than wolves. Kason will likely know who to contact. We can call him after we examine the remains," Aidon added.

That was sound advice. It was best to focus on one thing at a time. Before I knew it, we were pulling up outside what looked like an old warehouse. Stepping out of the vehicle, I scanned the area with my magic trying to detect anything that might be amiss. When nothing came back to cause alarm, we headed to the small door set into the façade of the building. We walked into a waiting area. Stella walked past the empty desk and through an open door. "They're set up in here."

I followed behind her, gaping at the sight in front of us. There were about a dozen people milling around four stainless steel tables. Some of them had bags of what I guessed was evidence while the rest surrounded one with a body on top of it. Energy of all kinds surrounded us making me light-headed.

A man that looked like he was in his mid-thirties glanced up and waved to us as he made his way toward us. He had piercing purple eyes and short brown hair that revealed his pointed ears. His tight black shirt hugged his slender frame while his cargo pants were loose on his legs.

"You must be Phoebe. I assume this is your mate, Aidoneus. And you must be Stella, her witchy partner. I'm Mohan. Thanks for coming." Unlike mundies, he didn't extend his hand for me to shake it. He turned and headed back to the victim.

Shaking my head, I hurried to catch up. "Yes, I'm Phoebe. What have you discovered?"

"We haven't learned much. The weapon was definitely enchanted. All I can say with certainty is that it is a Fae forged weapon of some kind. I recognized part of the magical signature," Mohan admitted.

I inhaled sharply as I got a look at the victim. She was killed while partially shifted. "I was leaning toward that when I looked at the last victim. I had hoped this one was killed by someone else. Unfortunately, the wounds are identical. I'd like to do a magical examination."

Mohan inclined his head and ushered his men away from the table. I glanced at Stella who stepped up next to me. I had to focus to push thoughts of the stench away. There was no mistaking the distinct smell of decay.

Stella and I had discussed using a reveal spell when we got here. Inhaling, I kept my intent to expose the killer and the weapon at the front of my mind, signaled Stella, then we chanted, "*revelare.*"

Energy trickled out of me and cocooned the victim before sinking into her skin. A buzzing sound echoed in my ears as our spell worked its way through the dead shifter. Her skin lit up green from within. An earthy scent drifted up toward us along with that of heated silver. An image of an ax flashed inside my mind.

Stella gasped and grabbed my hands. "Did you see that ax?"

I removed her fingers from my flesh. "I did. It was a Fae forged ax without a doubt. It had runes etched into the blade."

Mohan moved forward. "That has to be a dwarf. Axes are their weapons of choice. Did you get anything else, like the identity of the killer?"

A snort escaped before I could stop it. "If cases solved themselves that easily, I wouldn't be as busy as I am. What I do have is a sense of the person that made the weapon which is the best lead we've had yet."

"We should add that to the questions you have for the pixies. They're likely to know more about the dwarves that might have made such a weapon," Aidoneus interjected from his position crouched next to the victim.

I was feeling less and less hopeless as the day passed. My gaze skittered to the table of bags and my heart plummeted at the sheer number of them. That was a lot of evidence to go through.

Stella crossed her arms over her chest. "Do you know her name yet? We will need to contact her family right away."

Mohan nodded his head and picked up a sheet of paper. "Her name is Ellen Turner and I've already notified her family. Do you need anything else from her? If not, I will release her to her family."

I hesitated, wanting to tell him to hold onto her. Instead, I held up my hand and cast a spell to scan her for any foreign magic, DNA that didn't belong to her, or anything that might lead to her killer. The first pass came up empty, so I repeated it, focusing on trace evidence that might be helpful.

I sighed when I finished. "They can pick her up. There's nothing more I can get from her. Can your men deliver the evidence to the house where we are staying while we go and talk to the pixies?"

Mohan nodded his head. "I'd be happy to deliver them myself. I'll be around for the next couple days while we finish erasing evidence from the mundane system. Call if you need any assistance."

I assured the paranormal police agent that I would give him a call, then we left. My gut churned as sorrow over Ellen's death overwhelmed me. I let it course through me while we drove, not wanting to keep it under wraps when it was eating at me like this.

After a few minutes, I shook my head and refocused. "Okay, we need to pick up some lunch, which needs to include an energy drink, and head to the park."

Aidoneus lifted my hand and kissed the back of it. "Stella is way ahead of you. She called a restaurant that was featured on a television show. It will be ready when we get there. Are you alright, Queenie? This case is taking its toll on you."

I sighed and leaned my head on the seat behind me. "Dealing with death is never easy. I'm okay, though. Ready to find whoever is doing this. It would be worse if we didn't have next steps. I never understood how cases could go cold until now."

Stella sat forward. "You've got that right. I will never give Todd crap about not solving cases again."

Aidon pulled up to a familiar barbecue joint and parked in the curbside spot. "This place is good. You'll like it," I said with a smile.

We were on our way as soon as the food was brought out. For the second time in as many days, we were walking across the park and headed for the ley line on the far side.

I couldn't shake the feeling we were being followed. It was almost as if someone was spying on us and what we were doing. It made the back of my neck prickle.

Picking a spot close to the trees, I spread out the blanket I'd grabbed from the house and took a seat. Aidon and Stella joined me. As I was setting out the food, the sound of wings caught my attention. I nudged Stella and jerked my chin in the direction of the trees behind us.

Stella moved her big purse, setting it between us. "We need to find information about the two women who have been killed and are hoping you can help." She patted a spot on the blanket behind her bag where the pixies would be hidden from sight.

There were no people close enough to hear what we were saying so it would look like we were talking with each other. Aidon picked up a piece of pulled pork. "I am here to help my mate and mean you no harm."

The buzzing got closer before stopping as the pixie landed. "I'm so glad you're here and looking into this. I've heard about the Pleiades who mated a god of the Under-world. If anyone can find the one behind this, it's you guys."

I rubbed my arms. "We are trying our best. I'm Phoebe and this is my best friend, Stella and my mate, Aidoneus."

The pixie smiled up at me. "I'm Brialis. Good to meet you. Have you spoke with Thokrum Nightheart yet?"

Sweat beaded on my spine and rolled down into my butt crack. "No, we haven't heard of him. Who is that?"

The pixie's forehead furrowed. "He's the dwarf that made the ax being used in these murders. The ax was enchanted to give the wielder extra strength and was stolen from him shortly before these deaths occurred. He has been trying to follow its signature ever since."

I gasped then coughed as the meat in my mouth went down the wrong pipe. "How is that possible?"

Brialis sat down as Stella handed her a piece of a roll. "Dwarves are specialty craftsmen and their weapons are highly sought after. Most can't afford to have one created for them. Unfortunately, many try to steal them, so they started putting a spell on their weapons to detect when when they are used. It's the only way they can get them back. They remove the spell when they sell it to someone. Thokrum arrived too late to help the victims, so we suggested he call you in to solve the case. No way could we leave Mohan to do it."

My mind whirled a million miles a minute as I absorbed what she said. "That's precisely the information we needed to know. Can you put word out that we are in town and want to talk to Thokrum?"

Brialis nodded as she walked around the side of the purse to look over the food we had. Aidoneus used his body to block the sight of her from those in the park. "I'd be happy to ask him. I know he was hoping you could track the killer from the locations he left his victims. Come back tomorrow and I should have an answer for you."

I smiled at her still feeling like someone was out there watching us. "That's wonderful. And, thank you, for looking over my son when he comes to recharge. He told me he's seen you and your friends every time he comes here."

Brialis's eyes widened. "He's the one I saw you with yesterday? I will do everything in my power to ensure he stays safe."

"That would mean the world to me. He will be bringing a friend with him that I would appreciate being looked after, as well." I watched as the pixie picked through the food, stuffing bits and pieces in her mouth as she moved around.

Stella asked her questions, as did Aidon. She was startled when Tsekani arrived but didn't leave. She even gave her opinion on the clothes Tseki showed us. It was nice to sit in the park enjoying a meal without worrying about the next step. I left the others to talk while I ate and scanned the park, trying to locate our peeper. Unfortunately, I came up empty.

CHAPTER 14

*T*sekani swung his shopping bags in his hands as we made our way to the car. "Brialis brought up a good point. We need to go to the park where they found Edraele, then the place Ellen was located. I doubt Thokrum will have any faith in you without doing that. I know there is not likely to be any evidence to be discovered but you can tell him when he asks."

I'd been mulling over the exact same thing since the pixie made the comment. I'd dismissed the idea because it wasn't where the victims were killed. "I agree with you even though the likelihood of finding anything helpful is slim to none. From reports it seems as if very little time was spent in either location."

Aidoneus opened my car door for me and pressed a kiss to my lips before I climbed inside. "I'm not so sure about that, Queenie."

My brow furrowed as I watched him walk around the front of the vehicle. What was he talking about? Would there be a magical imprint on the space when all evidence pointed to the killer spending very little time in the location where the bodies were found?

"Oh!" It hit me as he started the car. "They were killed close to the dump site."

Aidon smiled at me then pulled out of the parking lot. "I knew you'd get it. If the dwarf followed the signature to the location where the ax was used, and it brought him to the location where the bodies were dumped, then it stands to reason he killed them close to where he dumped them."

Stella gasped behind me as Tsekani cursed. "It's so obvious now. I should have realized it the second Brialis told us about the enchantment on the weapon. The only reason the killer got away was because Thokrum was distracted by the victims. He was likely still nearby with the ax when Thokrum arrived."

Stella cocked her head to the side as she regarded Tsekani. "That actually makes sense. I was going to suggest we wait until dark, but doing a magical search won't be visible to any mundies nearby and it will give us time to check both locations before dinnertime. That way you can check on the kids without being torn between duties, Pheebs."

I sent her a grateful smile. It was nice having a friend that knew me so well and didn't hesitate to try and make my life easier. In the past I would wear myself out trying to accommodate everyone else. But these guys were always there to help shoulder my responsibilities.

I put the address into the map. "It might even be late enough in the afternoon that we encounter more dog walkers than anything else. Did anyone else feel like we were being watched back there, with Brialis?"

Aidoneus's head snapped in my direction and his eyes narrowed. "Why didn't you tell me you sensed something?"

I shifted my gaze to the screen on my phone as if I was

making sure we were going to the right place. "I'll take that as a no. I assumed I was being paranoid or that there were more curious paranormals nearby. It's not a big deal, it isn't as if we were hurt or anything."

I could feel Aidon's anger pulse around me. "Your powers will alert you to danger, Queenie. That could have been a warning. I would think by now that you would know better than to ignore something like that."

That last statement by Aidoneus triggered a brief trip back to my past. "I trusted that you would be able to protect me. I will mention it right away if it happens again."

"I think you might be right about it being people curious to see the Pleiades. Brialis didn't seem bothered and she lives in that park. If there was danger nearby, I would think she would know right away. Or her fellow pixies would," Stella postulated from the back seat.

Aidoneus turned down the street that would take us to the park where Edraele was found. To my surprise, it was one I used to take my kids to when they were little. "We shouldn't encounter too many in this park right now. Most moms are taking their children to activities at this time."

"We still need to be careful," Aidon replied. Clearly, he was upset with me. I'd have to make it up to him later.

I extended my hand and waited for him to take it. The tight coil around my chest loosened when he squeezed it before letting go to pull into the parking lot. The sun was low in the sky by the time we got out of the vehicle and headed toward the playground, where a family laughed and played.

"Where was Edraele found?" I whispered.

Tsekani pointed to our right, away from the jungle gym. "She was down that path a few feet and in the shrubs. I'll be able to pick up her scent when we get close."

Stella sucked in a breath and grabbed Tseki's hand as we

started walking. "If she was killed here then why didn't the shifters smell her somewhere else? They should have encountered her blood."

Tsekani's smooth forehead scrunched up as he scowled. "That's a good question. It's obvious the killer hid their actions magically somehow. The question is how precisely did they pull this off."

The energy surrounding us was far less than in the last park. And it had a sinister edge to it. We allowed Tsekani to lead us to the site where Edraele was located. I wasn't sure if it was knowing she had been left there, or something more, but a sense of dread permeated the air along with hatred.

Shivering, I watched as Tseki bent and pretended to smell the flowers. I moved closer. "Anything?"

Standing, he shook his head. "Nothing. Does the trail on the other side go further than this one?"

"No, this one has more trees than the other side. Although it isn't far until we reach the houses. This is a risky location," I observed. "Whoever did this was more likely to get caught here."

Stella cooed at a dog as it passed with its owner. "Or a location of convenience."

I did another quick scan to ensure we were alone, then extended my hands to Stella. It was easier to combine our magic when we had contact. I wanted this spell to spread as wide as possible as fast as possible.

Aidoneus watched us from the side. "I have some suggestions, if I may. Don't just focus on the blood when considering the spot where Edraele was killed. Concentrate on the evil that is necessary to take her life. It will give us a hint in the event they gathered the blood and removed it."

My stomach roiled and I gagged. "Can someone actually do that? It would have been on leaves, bark and soaked into the dirt."

Aidon grimaced. "Unfortunately, there are many beings that have the ability to gather every drop of blood from their surroundings. Most are demons, but they aren't the only ones."

I pressed my lips to his. "Thanks, Yahweh. Signal when you're ready, Stella."

Stella shifted her stance, tugging at my hands. She inclined her head and took several deep breaths. I copied her, focusing on uncovering the site of Edraele's murder and the associated malevolent energy. I concentrated on finding that bloodlust and lack of empathy.

I was ready by the time Stella dipped her head once. "*Revelare!*" The enchantment echoed around us.

Energy flowed from the two of us and spread out like a blanket over the area. My awareness prickled as it reached beyond the area we could see. My head began to spin at the same time orange sparks jumped along the ground on the other side of the park. Next to me Stella sounded like she was dry heaving. I was moving before I even realized what I was doing. The family playing on the playground, three kids and their mom hadn't missed what looked like fireworks.

One of the kids screamed for their mom and pointed in the opposite direction at the grey smoke that was flooding the area. It obscured the orange sparks which was good, but it smelled like old vegetables that had been soaked in vinegar for a few months.

The littlest child ran across the play area and fell when her feet reached the grey smoke. The mother set a little boy, around six years old, on the top of the slide then darted for her daughter, shouting her name. The oldest child, a girl around nine stood transfixed.

Aidoneus reached the little girl before the mom and scooped her up. I saw the fear in the mom's eyes. She had no idea if he was going to help her daughter or hurt her. I cupped my hands around my mouth. "It's alright. He's going to help her." Until he has to erase your memories. Guilt churned in my stomach with that thought.

Tsekani's nostrils flared. "You're Fae. Don't worry. This is the Pleiades. We're here to discover who killed Edraele the other night."

The mother sagged as the nine-year-old ran up to my side. "You're her? The Pleiades?"

I nodded my head. "I am and I'm here to make sure it's safe to play in your park."

The grey smoke was traveling further into the trees on the other side as were the orange sparklers. Nudging the little girl at the base of her spine, I gestured to the jungle gym with my chin. "Go play with your brother over there where it's safe."

The mother took her youngest from Aidoneus. There were tears in her eyes as she lifted them to mine. "It must be demons if you're here to solve this case. I had assumed it was Edraele's boyfriend. He gets jealous when guys hit on her and hates the fact that she works at a bar."

I placed a hand on her shoulder as I drew close to her. "There is no reason to panic but it would be wise to stay here and away from the hidden sections of the park until we discover what's happened."

The mother wrapped one arm around me. "I feel safe knowing you're on the case. If you can take on the master vampire and win, you can handle this no problem."

I smiled at her and hurried toward the grey smoke while trying not to scream. Handling Marius had been a necessity, but I hadn't expected this side effect from taking action against him. I didn't want to be hero worshipped. It just put pressure on me and built false expectations. There would be a time when I failed. What would they think of me then?

Stella grabbed my hand squeezing it. "Don't worry about

that right now. We need to find the location where she was killed."

My eyes burned the closer we got to that side. The smoke was so thick, I had to lift my sweater to keep it from choking me. It was impossible to breathe with the stuff surrounding us. There was a second where I became disoriented because I could hardly see in front of me.

A familiar hand landed on my shoulder, grounding me. Within a few feet we had passed through the smoke and were staring at the backs of houses. Turning, I ran into Tsekani's broad chest. He caught me by my arms. "It's in the middle of the smoke. We will need to clear it away to see anything."

A grimace twisted my features before I trudged back to the thick grey cloud. Stella suddenly jumped and threw a finger out. "There's movement inside the mist. The killer might be in there."

Without pausing, I rushed back into the smoke - and stopped short at what I saw. A movie was playing the attack out on the fog in front of us. My eyes blurred as they teared up, but I refused to clear the smoke away. It was channeling what happened to Edraele. I watched, stunned as she jogged past the playground and into the clearing where we were standing. There was no sound other than the crackle of the orange sparks at our feet, so I wasn't certain why she stopped running when she did.

Then Edraele spun in a circle, making her long blonde hair fly out around her head like a fan. A figure dressed in a dark colored hoodie walked out of the trees in her direction. "That is one small guy," Stella whispered.

"The ax is glowing blue," Tseki added.

We watched as Edraele scowled and pointed behind her. The hooded figure was a good half a foot shorter, but he was vicious. He lifted his arm and brought it down. Edraele tried to run away but the blade sunk into her arm. Her mouth opened and I wondered if she screamed. Someone should have heard her if she had made any noise.

I stood there, horrified. I felt helpless as I watched the killer bring the ax down two more times until Edraele fell to her knees. Her attacker took advantage and swung the weapon. The only thought that came to mind at that moment was that the killer seemed mindless or driven. There was no hesitation. I'd never seen anything so horrific in my life.

The blue glow of the ax blade was now almost entirely purple thanks to the blood coating it. Dark droplets flew in every direction with each arm movement. There should be blood everywhere. How the hell had the shifters missed that?

The killer paused with his hands in the air and watched as Edraele clearly struggled for breath on the ground. The weapon dropped to his side as he watched her die. The only indication that he'd just violently attacked someone was the way the killer's chest was heaving from the exertion.

Edraele's chest was still moving when the killer swiveled around. He crouched over her body and watched in the direction of the playground. I had no idea what startled him because we couldn't see it. After a few seconds, the figure stuffed the ax under his hoodie then lifted Edraele.

Even as she died, the elf tried to fight back and managed to grab hold of the killer's hoodie. I held my breath as I watched the cloth fall away from her attacker's face. My heart raced like a humming bird and my jaw went with it.

"What the actual fuck?" Tsekani's words echoed my thoughts perfectly.

I shot him wide eyes. "That tart killed her? But how?" I cringed when Miles's girlfriend punched Edraele in the face.

Aidoneus closed the distance, wrapping his arms around me. "Look, she's glowing."

I shook my head as I watched a faint light drift from

Edraele and move into the vile woman. I couldn't understand how that was even possible.

The tart walked away and the grey smoke disappeared the second the attack ended. I bent over and threw up the pulled pork I'd eaten not long before that. Aidoneus crouched next to me, rubbing my back as I dry heaved.

Stella paced next to us. "What do we do now?"

Aidon helped me straighten. "I have no freaking clue. This is bad. She's human, yet absorbing power from para-normals."

A million curses went through my head as I considered the improbability of what I'd just witnessed. The kids weren't going to believe what happened and Miles was going to throw a colossal fit. Unless he was somehow involved in this, too.

CHAPTER 15

*T*watched Stella setting food on the island at the kids' house while my mind continued churning Edraele's murder over and over in my mind. Aidon had suggested we cancel dinner with the kids, but I'd refused.

Jean-Marc knew me well enough to know I would be worried about Greyson and only something serious would keep me from visiting. I didn't want him asking any questions, so here we were. And I needed to snap out of it or I would alert Jean-Marc to my funk.

"Whoever you got to do the work in here did a great job, Tseki. And they were fast." Stella was grasping for safe topics of discussion, so the conversation didn't move to Miles and his murderous girlfriend.

Tsekani scanned the newly painted walls and cabinets. "It was a crew from Kason's pack."

"We should ask Sully if he has any construction workers in his pack. You're always saying you need reliable contractors for the homes you list, Stella."

Stella smiled as she continued unloading Styrofoam containers. "I was thinking the same thing. It would be nice to have them in cases where clients need special modifications that would be too difficult to explain to mundie workers."

Jean-Marc opened a container and snagged a piece of garlic bread. "I'm surprised Hattie didn't already have a system in place for that. She seemed to have one for everything else."

I sent my son a smirk. "She helped people buy homes all the time. There were several instances where she gave them money for the house and worked out repayment terms they could afford. She always did it through traditional means. And from what I've learned, she left anything else up to the owners once they took possession."

Stella turned to grab glasses from the cabinet behind her. "I'm creating a new type of business. Hattie focused on a singular need, such as being able to buy a home. The houses I look at often need a lot of work because they've been abandoned for one reason or another, creating multiple needs for one buyer."

Skylar approached the food with her plate in hand. "They're haunted, aren't they? How exciting. When we visit in a couple weeks can you take me to one? I've always wanted to see a ghost."

Stella and I shared a look then started laughing. Skylar dropped the calamari on her plate as she stared at us. "What?"

I shook my head. "Ghosts aren't always friendly, Sky. We just dealt with a poltergeist that practically killed an elf who bought the house."

Stella held up a finger. "Don't forget the sisters that threw us off their porch. They're why I got the idea to specialize in supernatural real estate. In the case of the sisters, they weren't a vengeful spirit like the poltergeist. They simply wanted witches to live in the house with them, not mundies."

"Actually, they didn't want any other type of supernatural to live there," Tseki pointed out.

Emmie filled her plate with some salad and grilled chicken. "How come you guys, and my mom, and Auntie Violet, and Aislinn face so many magical problems? Is it because you used to be a normal person? Will we start being attacked?"

I wrapped an arm around Emmie's shoulders, hugging her close. "You guys should be perfectly safe. As your power grows, you will want to be careful and mindful of those coming around. There are those that are jealous of the amount of power we have. Mine is different from your mom's but still highly sought after. Not to mention my position requires that I handle supernatural problems."

Emlyn cocked her head to the side. "Did your mom tell you that Phoebe is the Pleiades and what that means?"

Greyson nodded his head as he chewed a bite of steak. "She mentioned something about auntie being one of the most powerful witches alive."

"That's right," Emlyn replied. "Ms. Dieudonne` is one of seven Pleiades. They keep the peace in their areas. And oversee almost all of the magical world. Some, like the vampires, bristle at the oversight of a witch, even one as powerful as they are. However, without them, chaos would ensue and we would never have been able to remain secret from mundies."

"Did you ever think our moms would be these badass witches?" Jean-Marc asked Fiona's kids.

Each one of them shook their heads. It was Emmie who spoke. "Never in my wildest dreams could I have pictured us being supernatural. But I couldn't imagine better women to be in charge."

My mind traveled back to the issue of my ex-husband's trollop being a murderer. Dinner seemed to drag on as the kids' asked questions about various topics from what it was like to be a dragon to what kind of jobs were available in my company. Emmie was studying business and was interested in an internship. After happily arranging for Emmie to work with Lilith during their visit, we took our leave.

Aidoneus turned to me as he pulled away from the house. "I know that was difficult for you, and while I didn't agree with having dinner with them, I do see why you didn't want to cancel. They would have known something was up and pestered you about it. So, did you come up with any ideas of how to deal with this situation?"

I shrugged my shoulders, feeling the weight of the situation rest heavily upon me. "I want to ask her what the hell she's thinking before we have Mahon arrest her and put her in the Coldwater Correctional Facility. I still can't believe she killed someone, not to mention that she seems to be a paranormal. Did either of you sense she was supernatural when you met her at the bar the other day?"

Aidon shook his head. "Be careful not to act too hastily, Queenie."

I growled at him. "She must be some kind of an incubus to get you under her thrall, as well. So much for mating for life and loving me with your soul."

Stella gasped and Tseki hissed while Aidon held up a hand. "You are once again jumping to conclusions without pausing to consider all of the facts. I saw no indication that she was anything other than a human piece of trash, which got me to thinking about how she came into possession of a Fae weapon. And why she seemed to be possessed when she killed Edraele. Dark magic users can bespell identities among other things."

My face flushed with heat. "I'm sorry about that. Assuming you're right and the killer made herself look like

Miles's girlfriend we could be facing someone out to get me. That's the only reason they would use her likeness."

Aidon sucked air in through his teeth as his fingers tightened over the steering wheel. "The dark user might not have had her in mind at all. They might have left a spell in the area to mask their identity should anyone come looking for them."

"Are you saying that someone tapped into my and Phoebe's minds to come up with what the killer should look like? That sounds like an intricate and difficult spell," Stella surmised.

"Dark magic users are capable of more than you ever want to know." There was anger in Tsekani's voice making me think he was referring to Myrna, the witch that made him. "And that makes sense. Miles and his girlfriend have been at the front of your minds since Miles saw us at the ley line."

"You guys might be right about that, but I still want to go by the house and see if we can reveal her true identity. If she is a paranormal and is hiding it, we can discover that. My guess is she's trying to garner power by using the Fae ax to kill; kinda like the Tainted do with Blood magic." I don't know how she would have discovered the existence of witches and the like, but I wouldn't put anything past her.

Stella shook her head. "That's not a good idea. I say we go to the location where the police found Ellen and test Aidon's theory. If we picture someone specific and see them, it will confirm what we're dealing with."

I sighed and smiled at my best friend as I punched the location into the map. "Always the voice of reason. That's a brilliant plan. Who should we picture?"

Tseki sucked in a sharp breath. "What about Myrna? She's vile and capable of this type of murder and we know she's dead."

"She is a good one to test my theory because if Phoebe is right and Miles and his girlfriend are using a Fae artifact to garner power, we need to know about it. It shouldn't be possible, but Blood magic changes the playing field entirely," Aidon pointed out.

I snorted, thinking about who we were talking about. "Miles the assface and his tart changed things, as well. I'm going to think about how much shit Myrna put us through so I'm focused for this test."

"It doesn't take much to trudge up my anger toward that woman. She was awful," Stella replied in the backseat.

Myrna was an evil woman. I was about to talk about the Dark creatures she had surrounded herself with when the scenery caught my attention. "This is as populated as the last location. Whoever did this didn't care if they were discovered. You might be right, Aidon."

Aidoneus smirked at me as he parked the vehicle along the side of the road. "I usually am."

I chuckled not wanting to feed into his ego and scanned our surroundings. We were on a side street that ran along the back of some houses. There were about half a dozen large homes to our right with a green belt area to our left. I'd bet the shifter was killed in the trees and shrubs to the left.

I was about to cross the street when Aidoneus stopped me with a touch to my shoulder. "She was discovered in the bushes between these two houses."

Aidon pointed to a couple of houses halfway down the block. I looked around us, noting the fact that all but one of the houses was completely dark. Not a surprise given it was after ten o'clock at night.

"Where are we going to cast the spell?" Stella whispered in my ear.

Not near the house where the blue light of a television

glowed from an upstairs window. "Behind the vehicle. It'll shield us from that house over there."

All eyes tracked my hand to the house I was just considering. Moving into place, Stella and I clasped hands. I held my best friend's gaze and thought about Myrna while also focusing on discovering the location Ellen was killed.

I nodded to Stella and together we chanted, "*Revelare.*" The enchantment was whispered, yet we'd both poured a significant amount of energy into the spell.

Like before, energy flowed from the two of us and then traveled down the street. It touched on the area where Ellen was discovered and then moved across the street where it spread out like a blanket over the area.

My spine prickled as my senses picked up the power in the greenbelt area. My head spun and I tensed myself for the orange sparks and grey smoke. Aidoneus twined his fingers with mine as we headed across the street. Immediately, I smelled the vinegar-soaked rotten vegetables. It wasn't easier even though I was prepared for it this time. My eyes burned and watered the closer we got to that side.

Before we knew it, the smoke was so thick, we couldn't see through it. For the second time today, I lifted my sweater to keep from choking. I fought the disorientation as I clung to Aidon for support. Someone bumped into me and my hand shot out then grabbed hold of Stella. Tsekani grunted. "Where are you guys?"

"We're here," I called out. I had no idea how far we were into the greenbelt. If this was the same culprit, she would have done this far enough inside the area that she wouldn't be seen from the street.

Looking down, I looked for the orange sparks. A cluster of them gathered behind us. "There. We need to move back a bit."

We turned and headed back into the smoke. Stella went

to her tiptoes and then shook her head. "Maybe the orange sparks don't indicate the spot this time. I saw a large cluster back there, too."

My mouth opened to respond then snapped shut when movement in the fog caught my eye. A shiver traveled down my back as a menacing feeling overwhelmed me. Leaving the middle of the smoke, my eyes cleared. I saw Ellen walking down the path toward us.

The glint of silver flashed brightly in the dark smoke as the ax was swung by a disembodied arm. It slammed into Ellen's side. Black fur sprouted over Ellen's arms as blood dripped from her side. My gaze followed the crimson fluid but there was no sign on the path that any ever landed there. I looked up in time to see Ellen, partially shifted into her panther form, snarl then disappear as she headed toward the trees.

Aidon moved first, tugging me so we followed the shifter. We watched as she swiped her claws at her attacker who was wearing a dark hoodie pulled up over her head. I couldn't tell but she seemed taller than Miles's tart.

Ellen spun around and kicked out. The killer stumbled back, grabbing her side. Ellen took advantage and pounced on her. The attacker was prepared and swung the weapon overhead slicing Ellen's face open.

"The ax is glowing brown this time," Tseki pointed out.

I cocked my head to the side. "Is that because Ellen was a shifter?"

No one responded as we watched Ellen fall to her back. The killer jumped up making the hood fall back. I wasn't surprised to see Myrna this time. "Shit. You were right, Aidon. Now what?"

"We need to find out who is powerful enough to cast this type of enchantment while collecting the blood at the same time." Aidon cringed as the killer hacked at Ellen with the same mindless fury that we saw last time. It was as if she wanted Ellen terrified as she fought for her life.

Ellen put up more of a fight than Edraele and managed to injure her attacker, which only pissed the ax wielder off even more. Several more blows landed on Ellen before the shifter went still and returned to her human form.

The light that drifted from Ellen and into the vile woman was much lighter than last time. The killer was bleeding from several injuries as she stood up and kicked Ellen in the side.

I turned, and prepared for the scene to end, but that didn't happen. We watched the smoke spread across the street with the killer. Ellen staggered as she got to her feet. She put on a burst of speed, and partially shifted for a second time as she lunged at her attacker.

Ellen's hand wrapped around the ax as she fell into the bushes between the two houses where she was found. The killer made a move to grab it when a bright light shone on the scene that made her take off running.

"Holy shit. The police have the ax. That's what I felt at the police station when we visited the detective." I was shocked to say the least.

The smoke and sparks vanished, leaving us standing in the spot where Ellen was found a couple of days ago.

Stella's wide eyes lifted to mine. "She's going to try and get her weapon back. What do we do?"

I rubbed my eyes to clear the smoke from them. "We need to find the dwarf. I want him to confirm the ax is at the station before I go snooping around and raise mundie suspicion."

Aidon pressed his lips to my temple. "Talking with him is our best bet for sure. I could try and control the officers but it would require me to loosen the lid on my full powers which will be dangerous for the mundies."

Stella grimaced. "Let's not fry a bunch of police officers' minds. The pixies said they would get word to the dwarf. All we have to do is wait for him to come to us."

I shook my head. "I don't like the idea of waiting. The killer could kill policemen to get the ax back. And if the police don't have the ax, then the killer will probably strike again. The problem is that I have no idea where to find Thokrum."

Aidoneus shrugged his shoulders. "Dwarves live inside mountains. There are several nearby, but it's more likely that he will be hidden within range of that ley line juncture."

Tsekani's forehead furrowed. "That's a good place to start. However, he's not going to be too close, though because he'd be found easier."

Walking back to the rental car, I sighed as we hit yet another dead end. It seemed as if Miles's tart wasn't the killer, which was a good thing. Unfortunately, we were back to square one with our search which was frustrating as hell.

CHAPTER 16

I gratefully accepted the energy drink from Tsekani. "It's like you can read my mind."

Tseki snorted as he rolled his eyes. "I heard you grunting and groaning all night long. And not for any of the fun reasons, either. If we're going to tackle a mountain today, we need you on top of your game."

Stella smacked my arm. "You should have taken my bed. I can sleep on a firm mattress."

I grabbed her shoulders. "That thing goes beyond firm. It's a freaking rock. I'm having another mattress delivered today. No one can sleep on it."

Aidoneus leaned toward us. "I offered myself as her bed, but she denied me. Can you believe it?"

A laugh burst from Stella. "I honestly can't believe she turned you down. I would never turn Todd down."

I couldn't keep the smile from my face. "Shut it, you two. Are we ready for our trip up the mountain?"

Tsekani picked up some black leather boots that looked more like dress shoes than hiking boots, yet completely him. "I was thinking Stella and I should search one section while you guys' tackle another. There's a massive amount of land to cover and I feel the same urgency you do, Phoebe."

Shoving my feet into my worn leather boots, I considered his suggestion. My mind immediately went to the time Aidon and I had looked for Lilith in Mt. Batia. We ran into problems of the demonic nature and had to free her from a thrall. That trip had left me with countless injuries and nearly killed me, but it also had brought Aidon and I much closer together.

Experience told me that we shouldn't separate because bad things happened when we did. However, Tsekani was a freaking dragon that was capable of keeping both of them safe.

I made a face at him. "I don't like it but you're right. The odds of finding him are better if we can look through more area. But you'd better fly the two of you out of there at the first hint of trouble. This witch might be hanging out in the area hoping to steal another weapon from him."

Stella handed me a small backpack filled with water and snacks then grabbed hers. "I'll make sure he gets us out of there. Or I might just have him incinerate her where she stands."

Chuckling, I grabbed the jacket I had packed at the last minute, then locked the door behind us. Aidon looked at me with one brow raised. I returned the expression. "What? If we're out there when it gets dark, I'm going to get cold."

Aidoneus wrapped me in his arms and pulled me into his body. "I'll keep you warm."

Before I could answer, he pressed his lips over mine and kissed me senseless. My arms wound around his neck and my body became putty in his embrace. The man was dangerous for my sanity. With one touch he never failed to ignite my desire. His lips made that arousal explode like a volcano.

The honking of a horn made me jump away from Aidon. I swiveled and sent my best friend a scowl. Unapologetically, she tapped her wrist from the back seat and waved us on. Sticking my tongue out at her, I got in the passenger seat.

"You should have taken him up on his offer last night. A night of hot sex is a far better reason to lose sleep than a hard mattress," Stella said.

A sigh escaped me. "Dammit, I hate when you're right. Maybe I won't have that mattress delivered today."

Aidon waggled his eyebrows then backed out of the driveway. "I'm good with that."

Tseki patted Stella on the arm. "You and I need to go out tonight. It's been too long since I had sex and I bought the perfect shirt yesterday. It makes my eyes even greener. Guys will fall all over me."

"No one is going anywhere unless we find this dwarf," I corrected them.

Tseki lifted his chin in the air. "That's alright. There are bound to be guys on that mountain. I won't be alone for long."

I chuckled as we settled in for the hour-long drive. Looking out the window, I watched the scenery as we passed and thought about how busy my house was going to be in a couple of short weeks.

Thankfully, Nimaha was big enough to house everyone. It would be nice for Nina to have the other kids around. She was the youngest of their group and always wanted to be part of whatever they were doing. As teenagers, they hadn't wanted her tagging along. It would be different now that she was almost seventeen.

That reminded me her birthday was coming up soon. I needed to call the Six Twisted Sisters and have them come out and do her party. Or maybe we would go back to New

Orleans for a visit. I knew the kids would love to see the city, and I wanted to see more of it myself.

"Ready, Queenie?" Aidon's voice startled me.

I hadn't realized we had arrived already. "Oh, yeah. I was just thinking I need to have the Smith sisters do a party for Nina. Don't let me forget. The divorce took her Sweet Sixteen and I refuse to allow these magical problems to take any more from her."

The air was cooler when we got out of the car making me glad that I brought my jacket. Aidon took the backpack from me and wrapped the coat through the straps. "I will be sure to remind you, Queenie."

Tsekani lifted his phone. "We aren't likely to get cell service out here. Can you ask Tarja if she can act as a go between in the event, we need to talk to one another?"

I nodded and reached out to my familiar who responded right away. "*I would be happy to relay information as needed, Phoebe. And, I am proud of how you have handled this investigation thus far. Be careful today. Dwarves can be nasty little critters when they're upset and if Thokrum's ax was stolen, he's going to be very upset.*"

"*I wasn't sure how much you'd been checking in on us.*" I felt like I needed to explain why I hadn't needed to reach out to her for help like I usually did which was ridiculous.

I didn't need to make excuses for knowing what I was doing. There had been more times than not when I'd had no clue about how to handle a situation and I knew there'd be many more. Tarja was there to help me when needed and add her power if it became necessary. She wasn't a crutch for me but a friend.

"*You're doing wonderful. I'm here should something come up and the ley lines should make communicating easier.*"

Thanking Tarja, I turned my attention to my friends.

"She's happy to be our telephone. I'll check in with you guys in a few hours. Be careful."

Stella hugged me, promising to watch for danger before they left. Aidoneus and I went in the opposite direction. I scanned our surroundings, taking in the trees and plethora of ground cover. "I think we should move higher and do this in reverse. I doubt his cave will be down this low."

Aidon tilted his head then shrugged his shoulders. "The entrance to his cave might not be right here, but I believe Thokrum is more likely to be closer to this area."

Together, we turned to look up the mountain before we started climbing. As comfortable as they were, my boots weren't made for hiking. Within a few feet, I was cursing my decision to go straight up and then wind our way back down.

I grabbed onto a tree and pulled myself up a particularly steep section. "I take it back. We can do this your way."

Aidon chuckled, not out of breath in the least. "No, your suggestion actually makes a lot more sense. He would not have made the entrance obvious, nor would he have made it so close to the energy surge. Too many paranormals venture through that section."

There was no way to continue a conversation as we climbed. At one point, Aidon went to one knee in front of me. His back was to me and he glanced over his shoulder at me.

"Your chariot awaits, mi' lady." His smile made me swoon.

"And what a fine ride it is," I teased as I climbed on his back.

He stood, holding onto my thighs. It was much better to have a piggyback ride. I enjoyed not having to climb the steep incline for about half an hour. The journey was so uneventful that I let my attention go lax. That was when things went to shit. A blur in the corner of my eye caught my attention. I turned in time to see an animal heading directly for us.

"Wolf," I screamed into Aidon's ear.

It was too late. The creature hit his side and the three of us went flying. Aidon's grip on my thighs vanished and I sailed into a tree trunk. The breath was knocked out of me as I slammed into the bark. It stunned me long enough that I landed on my face, unable to get my hands up in time to break my fall.

Aidoneus roared as he kicked the wolf. The massive creature had to weigh a ton because it hardly moved when Aidon's foot connected with its torso. The two of them grappled in a flurry of snarls, fists, and claws.

They were like a whirling dervish, moving so fast I could barely keep track of them. It gave me time to gather myself and get to my feet. Unfortunately, I wasn't able to concentrate on either of them enough to cast a spell to stop the altercation.

In a burst of power, Aidoneus's wings ripped from his back and flared out to the sides. The echo of his energy hit me in the chest. It warmed me even as it shocked the wolf. The way his power seemed to envelop me told me that I would be safe even if he showed me his true self. The urge to test that theory overwhelmed me for a split second. That brief flash of his strength gave me a glimpse of what he meant when he said he couldn't unleash all of himself without harming others. I wasn't willing to take a chance with my life like that. But I made a mental note to have a conversation with him later.

The wolf staggered as it stood up. Aidoneus made a move toward it. I placed a hand on his shoulder, making him pause, then turned my attention to the animal. "We aren't here to harm anyone or steal anything. We're trying to solve two murders."

The wolf looked between us, shook its head then stalked off, leaving us staring after him. Aidon shrugged his shoulders and his wings disappeared. "Do we follow him?"

Cocking my head, I gasped when I saw he was covered in cuts and bruises. I rushed to his side. "Holy shit, are you alright? Some of them look bad."

He shook his head as he looked at me with a half-smile. "I'll be fine, Queenie. You don't have to worry about me. I'm a god, remember?"

I rolled my eyes as I probed the edges of a wide gash on his arm. "I would stitch this if I had supplies. And just because you're a god doesn't mean you're impervious to death, does it? If you bleed, you can die."

Aidon shot me a look that was part shock, part wonder. "No one has ever worried about whether I can die or not. To answer your question, I can be killed, but it will take significantly more than a wolf to do so."

That made sense. Although, I was surprised a god could be killed at all. "Good to know. But you can still be hurt and I worry about you."

Aidon pressed his mouth to mine briefly. "I love you, too, Queenie. Now, let's find the ax's maker."

I took a deep breath, not looking forward to the search. "Let me try a tracking spell. I need to concentrate on the maker of the ax."

Aidoneus nodded as I pulled up an image in my mind of the ax, concentrating on the hands that forged the metal and etched the runes into the blade. *"Promo."*

My magic exploded out of me much like the last time I was at the ley line. The boost of being close to the nexus of energy amplified my spell. I could feel it soaking into the soil and spreading out around us.

My senses were hit all at once by a myriad of details. There was a bear shifter in the mountains, and the wolf that had attacked us was a shifter, as well. There were some brownies and wood nymphs but no dwarf. To my surprise, I was getting a hit on the other side of the hill.

"He's on the other side," I told Aidon as I reached out to Tarja.

"I've already told Stella and Tsekani. They haven't found a cave opening, yet though."

"The signal I'm getting isn't underground. And it is located close to the base of the mountain. He could be returning. Let them know we are heading their way now."

"They have refocused their search," Tarja informed me.

I relayed the news to Aidoneus as he hitched me onto his back and hurried around the side of the mountain. I guided him as we moved. It wasn't long before I saw Stella and Tsekani.

"We haven't found anything yet," Stella called out when she saw us up the incline from her.

My forehead furrowed. The signal had shifted. "He's getting further away now."

Tsekani gestured below us. "Do we go down?"

I tapped Aidoneus's shoulder for him to put me down. Once on my feet, I spun in a circle. "I'm not sure. Let's move closer to the nexus. Hopefully, the power there will boost my spell."

It took fifteen minutes to reach the section where Greyson and Jean-Marc had recharged their energy stores and lodestones the other night. Once there, my enchantment seemed to have fizzled.

The signature was bouncing in and out of focus which was highly confusing. "I need to recast the tracking."

Stella grabbed my hand. "Let's do it together."

I agreed and told her the spell I used earlier. It was easier for me to find my focus a second time, so I was ready when Stella squeezed my hands a few seconds later. Our enchantment flowed from us in a wave of blue light, like a damn bursting from within us. There was more energy behind the spell this time, but it was smoother as it left us and spread out. The light immediately narrowed to a line that moved to the left of where we were standing.

Tsekani made a surprised noise. "That's convenient."

I chuckled as we followed the trail created by our magic. "Do you feel him?" I asked Stella as my senses picked up a strong signal down a different slope in the opposite direction from where Tseki had been pointing earlier.

Stella cocked her head to the side. "No, I don't."

I was in the processing of pondering if the difference was due to my having more power when we saw smoke. "There," I pointed.

Stella and I were practically running to keep up with Tseki and Aidon as they took off to investigate the smoke. We came to a small clearing and discovered a short man with long, dark brown hair, and a beard that made him look like he belonged in the musical group ZZ Top, standing on the porch of a small cabin.

He stood up from the rocking chair he was sitting in and waved. "Yes, I'm Thokrum. Thank you for coming to help me, Phoebe Dieudonne`."

Not what I expected when we set out to find the dwarf. He might have gotten my name from the pixie, but that wasn't a guarantee. Grabbing Stella's arm, I hesitated in our approach. This seemed too easy. We could be surrounded by magical booby traps. No way was I going in blind.

CHAPTER 17

I focused on our environment and sent out a tendril of my magic. The dwarf leaned against one of the posts on his porch and crossed his arms over his chest. "Once you're done with your scan, would you like some tea?"

It wasn't a surprise that he'd felt my probe and I didn't apologize. Considering his offer, I shook my head. "No thank you. Why don't you have stronger wards? Or any booby traps?"

The others followed when I resumed the trek to the dwarf's door. Aside from some basic protections, nothing protected the dwarf's home. I hardly noticed them as we crossed onto his property.

I picked up several powerful signatures inside his house which made the lack even more surprising. They had to be weapons that he'd created.

Thokrum's expression went from friendly to angry in a flash. "Because whoever took my ax destroyed the protections I had in place, leaving me defenseless. It's why I couldn't come to you. I can't leave my house like this. There's too much at stake."

Now that he mentioned it, I could feel the residue of whoever shattered his wards. Shaking my head, I focused on the signature, trying to get a sense of the magic user. I couldn't tell if it was a Tainted witch, but assumed it had to be.

No Light witch would break in and steal an ax then enthrall a woman to kill a couple of powerful supernaturals. I glanced at Stella. "Can you get a sense of the magical signature? I'm only getting bits and pieces."

She closed her eyes for several seconds then shook her head from side to side. "I can't get anything aside from what remains of the wards."

Aidoneus rubbed the back of his neck. "Neither can I."

I had a few items from the murder scene I could try to use to scry and track later. I turned to Thokrum and introduced the others. "You help us track down the person responsible for these murders and my friend and I will cast new protection wards around your place. Speaking of which, I was under the impression dwarves preferred to live inside mountains."

Thokrum shrugged his shoulders before opening his front door. "I'd appreciate the help. I have my brother out looking for a witch to hire. As to why I live out here, I like the open air. Not to mention being out here allows me to access the magic at the ley line nexus. I can't do that beneath the mountain. There's too much silver in the way. Staying cleaner is a bonus."

I glanced at his filthy hands hating to think how much dirtier he would get if he lived inside the mountain. We followed as he entered the house. What looked like a small cabin from the outside was anything but on the inside.

It was dark, which I expected given the few windows, but the interior was big. It almost reminded me of a shotgun house in New Orleans. I could see all the way from the front door to the back door down a long hall.

The entrance opened into a living room to the right where a sofa and television were located and a library on the left that had one chair along with bookcases along all four walls.

Thokrum was halfway down the hall when I looked away from the books. There were three open doors ahead of us. The first was a room that had one long table where weapons of various kinds were located. There were shelves lining two walls with herbs of some kinds. The hum of power I felt outside was coming from this room. I couldn't see if they were marked with runes or not.

It wasn't important to investigate those more closely at the moment, so I continued along with the others. I felt the heat from the third room when I paused to look at the platform bed in the second room. The room itself was neat as a pin. There was nothing on the bedside table aside from a lamp and nothing at all on the dresser.

I was more interested in the third room, where I suspected he kept his forge. My eyes widened as I took in the open back wall. Stella and I shared an amazed look. I was certain my expression matched her incredulous one.

There was a large fire pit in the corner of the space with a barrel of water next to it. There was an anvil with a hammer next to that. Metal, tools, and too many other things to count littered other surfaces in the room. My gaze skipped from the smoke-stained ceiling to the clearing outside.

Thokrum doubled back when he noticed we hadn't moved. "I made the walls retractable. This place would be unbearable if this room didn't open up to the woods."

"Not sure I could live like this. I'd be too afraid of bears or coyotes," Stella said with a shiver.

Thokrum shrugged. "Animals and I have a good relationship."

I wiped a bead of sweat that rolled down my forehead. "Why didn't you leave your name when you called me to tell me about the murder? You asked for help but didn't give us anything to go on."

Thokrum averted his gaze then continued down the hall. The kitchen was in the back of the house where the other door was located. The space looked like any modern kitchen with stone countertops, a stove, and a refrigerator. I moved to the wooden table and took a seat as the dwarf got flavored mineral water from the fridge and popped the tab.

"I was afraid. This thief used my ax to kill people and they altered my runes. I was busy trying to figure it out at the first scene so I didn't get to the second one as fast as I would have liked. I had no idea police had been called and didn't see anything amiss in the area. I should have stuck around but after hearing what you did to the vampires, I was afraid you would think I was guilty."

Aidoneus, Stella, and Tsekani had taken seats with me. Aidon leaned forward in his chair. "What do you mean your runes were altered?"

I wanted to know that, too, but was too busy reeling from the fear in his voice when he talked about what I did to Marius and his clan. My message was definitely affecting the magical community. I just hoped it was scaring the vamps as I had intended.

The dwarf, who had remained standing, shivered. "I have no idea. All I can tell you is that the ax has a different feel to it now. It was why it took me longer to recognize the signal the first time it was used."

How the hell had someone altered the runes? And what did it mean?

"Can you locate the weapon when it's not in use?" I asked. If he could then we could locate the killer.

The dwarf shook his head. "Not unless I'm in close proximity to it. The magic in the weapon needs to be activated for me to sense it from anywhere."

A thought hit me when he said that. I'd felt a similar signal to his weapons in the police station when we were there and told him what I had experienced. "Do you think you would be able to tell if it was in there?"

One of Aidoneus's perfectly shaped eyebrows arched to his hairline. "You think the killer dropped the ax when killing Ellen? I doubt they would just leave without it."

Stella pointed at Aidon. "Unless they had no choice. The mundies came out of the house. Remember in the scene we saw? I swear she lost it during that altercation."

"I was thinking the same thing," I replied.

The dwarf drained his mineral water and crushed the can between his palms. "I will know the second I step inside the building, if it's in there."

I rubbed my hands together. "Alright then. Let's cast some protections, Stella, so we can take Thokrum on a road trip."

Tseki stood up. "Be sure to close them and tune them to Thokrum. That way no one can get on his land without his permission."

The dwarf's eyes lit up. "I would be happy to pay you for that service. I have my brother looking for a witch to do just that. It's the only way I can be sure no one will be able to crack them again when I'm not home."

I'd never done anything like that. How the hell did I accomplish that one?

"You can do that easily. Think of the wards like a room with a locked door and the dwarf is the key to that room." My familiar came through for me once again. And I suspected it was

draining her to be in such close contact with me because her voice sounded weak.

"*Did you tell Stella, too?*"

Tarja's familiar scratchy laugh echoed in my head. "*I did. And you do not need to worry about me. I am fine for now. It will become harder as the kittens develop and require more energy. I am here when you need me, but you are doing a fantastic job without me. I'm sure you would have come up with the solution if you'd given yourself time to consider it.*"

Stella tilted her head to the side. "Ready?"

Shaking my head, I smiled at her. "Yes. I am. We can do this outside on our way to the car."

I led the way out of the house and paused with Stella at my side in what passed as the dwarf's yard. His home was built between trees with the back extending into a clearing. Nothing signified where his property ended, so I felt around for the previous ward and used that as a guide then pictured a house with a locked door dropping on top of it.

Stella clasped my hand and squeezed it. Together we chanted, "*protego.*"

Once again, the magic flowed like white water rapids from us. This time the light that accompanied it was purple. It settled over the area in a blocky building that rose two stories above the cottage. Steam rose from the ground when it hit the dirt.

Thokrum spun in a circle with a huge smile on his face. "I knew you were talented and powerful but never expected this. Thank you!"

I patted the short man on his shoulder. "You can thank me by coming to the police station and telling me what you feel."

Thokrum nodded and followed us to the rental car. Thank the gods Aidoneus preferred a large SUV to a sedan or we would have needed to rent another vehicle during this trip. We'd carted more people around than I had anticipated.

I'd been slightly fatigued after casting the protections around Thokrum's house but was rejuvenated as we passed through the nexus. Before I knew it we were in the car and heading back into town.

"We should reach the station after most have gone home which will make it easier for the five of us to walk inside," Aidon said as he drove.

I put my hand on his leg. "What if the detective has gone home? Then who do we ask to talk to? That might be a problem."

Aidon shrugged his shoulders. "We will cross that bridge when we get there. I can always use more power on the receptionist. Besides, I will only need to get you in the back. If Thokrum senses the ax, it will most likely be in the section where they store the evidence."

I gasped and put a knee on the seat, so I was facing him. "Maybe we don't need to go after all. Mahon was supposed to destroy all evidence."

Tsekani shook his head from side to side. "It's more than likely that Mahon's cleaners are still erasing memories. They do that first before moving to physical and electronic evidence so no one knows if it goes missing. Locating all of the humans and handling them takes time and it's only been a day since they arrived in town."

I sighed, feeling my shoulders relax. "It feels like it's been longer since we got here."

Stella laughed. "That's because we packed a week's worth of work in the two and a half days we have been here."

The dwarf shifted in his seat between Stella and Tseki. "I admit I was shocked you arrived at my place so quickly. Oh, it might be close. When you turned onto this street, I got an alert."

"The police station is half a block away," Stella pointed out. "You might not even need to go inside."

I sincerely hoped he could tell us from the parking lot. It would make dealing with the receptionist and detective easier. "Tell us as soon as you feel anything stronger. I'm going to make myself invisible before we go inside. It will be easier to make my way back to the evidence room if none of the mundies know I'm there."

Stella stuck out her lower lip. "I want to be invisible, too."

"I need you with Aidon, especially if Thokrum needs to join us inside," I told her. It wasn't that I didn't trust her abilities, she was a natural at witchcraft. I didn't want her caught if something went wrong. It would be easier to get just me out, rather than both of us.

The corners of her mouth turned down as she nodded her head. "Alright. I'll help Aidoneus, even though he's a god and can do this without me. I can just stay in the car. That would be even easier."

I'd hurt her feelings. "We need you inside. If something happens to me, you're the only one that can retrieve the ax. Aidon will need to keep control of the mundie minds."

Barely mollified, she nodded then jumped out of the car the second Aidon parked. I joined her and nudged her shoulder. She waved a hand at me. "I'm fine. I'm just used to always being at your side throughout it all. Let's do this. Can you tell if it's inside, Thokrum?"

I loved my best friend. She was right. She'd been with me through thick and thin. Despite the time we'd spent apart over our lives; she was still my ride or die and that was priceless.

The dwarf closed his eyes as he faced the building. His lids flew open a second later. "It's in the back of the building. Southeast corner."

Finally, we got a break. I scanned the area around us.

"Which side is that? I'm turned around out here."

Thokrum pointed to the opposite side of the building. "Over there. It's definitely the ax. I can feel my energy signature along with the changed magics."

"Good. That makes it easier. I'll stay here with Thokrum that way there are only Aidon and Stella to contend with," Tsekani suggested.

I clapped Tseki on the shoulder. "Keep your eyes peeled in case the killer shows up. I have a feeling she will want the weapon back."

Tsekani assured me he would be on guard. I cast my invisibility spell and followed Aidon and Stella to the police station. There was a different receptionist from the last time we were there.

This mundie had an easier mind to manipulate because Aidon and Stella were led right back. I branched away from them going down a different hall so I could locate the evidence locker.

I passed a couple of offices and the restrooms. There were double doors at the end of the hall that needed to be accessed via a keycard. My heart was pounding against my rib cage and I couldn't catch my breath. I'd never done anything like this before.

For some reason stealing from the police department was a lot harder for me than killing demons and vampires. Taking evidence was wrong, yet I still had to do it. My hand went to my chest as I panted and tried to slow my heart.

I needed to get through those double doors and keep quiet or I was going to be discovered regardless of being invisible. I should have also cast a silencing spell to mask any noise I made. It was too late now. I couldn't concentrate on shit.

I was sneaking into the evidence locker and was blocked by a couple of locked doors. There was a tan square on the wall that I was used to waving my ID over in the hospital. Crap, I needed to see if one of the other doors was an office. I was about to search for an ID when Detective Richardson pushed open the panels. I darted between them when he passed me while holding my breath.

There was a cage about five feet in front of me with a guy sitting behind a desk. My chest was burning as I still held my breath. I couldn't let him hear my panting. My lungs burned as I searched for a way into the cage.

That was where I needed to go. The magic was stronger on that side of the doors and concentrated behind the guard. It was in the caged area without a doubt. I needed to get back there but had no way of doing that without distracting the officer.

I went back to the double doors, hoping I didn't need a keycard for this side. I was in luck because I didn't see a tan panel. Kicking the door open, I ran back to the evidence area and ducked inside when the guard came out.

I sucked in oxygen as my vision started to go blurry. Running up and down the first aisle, I was just entering the second when the guard returned. The ax was sitting on a shelf, halfway down the aisle. I rushed and grabbed it when the cop shouted at me. "Stop. Who are you and what are you doing back here?"

I froze with the ax lifted to my side. I had no idea I had lost control of my invisibility. I was too scattered to cast at the moment. No way was he going to allow me to walk out with the weapon.

"I'm sorry," I told him as I raced at him. He reached for the gun in his holster. Thankfully, I had a leg up on him and was able to slam the end of the ax down on his head.

I winced as he crumpled to the floor. "Shit, shit, shit. What did I do?"

I knelt down and felt his pulse then checked to see if his

head was bleeding. His pulse was racing and there was a lump forming but he wasn't bleeding. He could have a subdural hematoma. I hated leaving him lying there without getting him help.

I got up and ran from the cage and was in the hall a second later. Loud voices caught my attention making me duck into the first room I came to along the hall. The urinals along the wall when I walked in told me I was in the men's bathroom.

Not the place I wanted to be stuck. I ducked into one of the two stalls and got up on the seat. I took deep breaths, focusing on making myself silent and invisible. I opened my mouth to cast the spell when the door burst open. "Bathroom's clear," shouted a male voice. I thought I was going to have a heart attack.

This was the craziest situation I had ever been in. And I felt like shit was spiraling out of control. I was going to be caught and thrown in jail. They would discover my magic and the government would study me in a lab.

Enough, Pheebs! Get your crap together and calm the hell down. I exhaled when the door closed and held the ax down at my side. Closing my eyes, I concentrated on what I needed to cast my spell. It took several seconds before I was able to concentrate. *"Tacet et invisibilia."*

The enchantment barely left my lips when the door opened again. Two guys walked inside, one of whom was Detective Richardson. The stall door where I was standing opened, but the uniformed officer paused before entering it to look back at the detective. "How can you be so calm when someone broke into the evidence locker?"

I slipped past the officer as the detective unzipped his pants. I had no desire to stick around and watch him pee but I couldn't get out without raising suspicion. Richardson turned and started peeing while he replied to the officer. "I think Simons hit that alarm by accident. He can't tell us why he pushed the button and nothing was missing from the locker. Not to mention it's impossible to get back there without an ID. I personally think Simons is drinking again. Wouldn't be surprising since that's what got him stuck back there."

The uniformed officer shrugged his shoulders. "I hope you're right. They're running a thorough inventory just to be certain."

My heart was pounding so hard it was about to jump out of my chest. I couldn't believe I was stuck in a men's bathroom with stolen evidence while trying to maintain an invisibility spell during a major freak out. This was going to bite us in the ass because I had messed up. My panic was rising when the bathroom door opened again.

Aidoneus strolled inside and greeted the officer and detective. Their expressions went slack. The tight band around my chest vanished and I sucked in a much-needed breath.

"Queenie, are you in here?" Aidon whispered the question.

"Yes," I shouted before realizing he couldn't hear me. Placing my hand on his arm, I tugged him out of the room. I don't know what I did to deserve such a great guy, but I thanked the fates for bringing him into my life.

He pulled me in front of his body as he walked out of the police station. "That was close. What the hell happened? I had to wipe too many minds at once in there and left most of them with no explanation for the missing chunk of time."

I squeezed his hand, not willing to drop the invisibility or silence until we were well away from the front of the police station. I leaned on Aidon as we walked because my pounding heart and short breaths were making me dizzy. God bless it, that was way too freaking close for my liking.

CHAPTER 18

There was a commotion behind us as several police officers filed out of the building at the same time. Aidon cursed as he paused. "I'd better deal with them. I thought we could get away with leaving things open ended."

I dropped the invisibility and silence spells, then laughed and placed a hand on his chest. "We're dealing with cops. There is not a more suspicious bunch on the planet. They see the worst of humanity and deal with assholes, so they don't trust anything. Especially holes in their memories. At least you didn't fry their brains and erase everything they knew."

Aidoneus pressed his lips to mine, lingering a second longer than was prudent given the police had noticed us. I sighed and broke away from him. My need to kiss the life out of him didn't matter at the moment. He needed to curtail any further questioning of who we were and why we were in the parking lot so close to the building.

"I'll be right back," Aidon promised before he darted back to the police officers.

I continued to the car that was parked at the back of the lot. Given the large bulge at my back, I decided to stick to the shadows as much as possible. I ducked behind a large van as headlights from a vehicle pulled into the parking lot.

No sooner had I gone to my knees than I was hit with the feeling of ants crawling across my skin. It was nauseating as all get out. Scanning the area, I searched for the black energy now trying to smother me. My gaze went to the vehicle that had just pulled into the lot. But all it did was turn around and pull back onto the street.

Staying low didn't give me a good view of everything in the parking lot. Needing to take the chance, I lifted until I was just able to see across the hood of a nearby sedan. My breath caught in my throat as my eyes landed on a dark-haired woman walking toward the front of the building. Following her gaze, I watched as Aidoneus led the officers back inside the station.

"Who are you and why do you have my weapon?" The voice was gravelly and far deeper than should come out of a short woman that might weigh a hundred pounds soaking wet.

"*Stella and Thokrum are coming up behind you to offer their support. Do not let this witch touch you. She doesn't feel right.*" Hearing Tarja inside my head startled me for a second.

Gathering myself, I took my time standing up. "Is she Tainted? *Tell Stella to mask their presence so Thokrum can grab the ax if necessary, without alerting our visitor.*"

"*I feel Dark energy around her but her magical signature isn't Tainted. I've never experienced anything like it. Stay on guard.*"

"I don't have anything of yours," I replied as I remained right where I was.

The witch turned to fully face me. She was building energy to cast a spell. Shields were second nature for me by now and I cast one around my body without much effort or concentration.

"That pathetic barrier will not protect you for long. I'm

more powerful than you can imagine. You will not take the power I found. Not many know the secret of getting more magic without Turning and I'm not willing to share. That weapon is mine and I want it now." The witch moved closer to me as she continued her diatribe.

There was obvious power suffusing the ax but I had no idea where it came from. I assumed it was thanks to the dwarf's runes. I moved forward a couple of steps in reaction to the witch before I caught myself.

I scoffed as I rolled my eyes. "There is no way to take from another without becoming Tainted and given the two people you have killed, you skipped Tainted and went Dark. Blood magic leaves an indelible mark on your soul. And trust me, you feel evil."

The witch's face turned red, her fists clenched at her sides, while she took deep breaths and tried to calm herself down. The next thing I knew, she was flying toward me. She was a good actress because I didn't have any hint that she was going to make a move.

I twisted, trying to avoid her. Her chest hit the side of my shoulder and her hand immediately went to my back. My flesh stung as she scratched me, ripping my sweater. Her fingers wrapped around the handle of the ax making the power in the runes flare to painful life.

I cried out when it burned my lower back at the same time, I threw my elbow into the witch's stomach. Pain radiated down my legs, weakening them. My energy reacted automatically and flowed to the injury.

Stella and Thokrum moved from the shadows behind me and raced for us. The witch pulled her hand and the weapon away from me, but it was still under the fabric. Shout out to designer brand clothes because despite the hole the blade had cut into the fabric, it didn't tear anymore. Tseki would be unbearable when I told him how the top held up in battle.

The witch tossed a ball of fire at Stella and Thokrum as she yanked hard on the weapon. A pulse of earthy energy flowed from the weapon and into me, energizing me. The power wasn't anything like mine, but it was light and boosted my efforts to get free. Wrenching myself out of the witch's grasp, I ducked down and got kicked in the side of the head. The blow made stars dance in my vision right before the top of my skull slammed into the side panel of the vehicle. The sound of metal bending was loud in my ears and had me worrying the police would hear it and come running.

Stella joined the fight as she screamed and tossed fire back at the witch. Where the thief's flames had been orange, Stella's were the pink of her witch fire. The witch was as nimble as a cat and evaded the flames making them hit a vehicle close to the front of the building. Turned out it was a cop cruiser. Stella put the pink flames out a second after the vehicle erupted.

Thokrum helped me stand up. "Tsekani went to check the back of the building when I sensed the same magical signature as I did after the ax was stolen."

Lifting my top, I took the weapon from my jeans before the witch got her hands on it and handed it to the dwarf. "Protect this with your life. Do not let her get a hold of the thing."

Thokrum's arm vibrated when he accepted the ax. The silver glowed in the night as his runes glowed blue on the blade. "I won't let anyone take it." Power bounced through the air around the dwarf, making me suck in a breath. He was packing some serious abilities. "This is charged with foreign energy. Taken by force. The runes are doing something to it."

I turned to help Stella when Thokrum called out. "Phoebe, that witch wasn't the one that stole the ax. It was another and I felt their magic in the back of the police station."

Tsekani was back there investigating, but he might not be able to handle it on his own. *"Tarja, ask Aidon to help Tseki behind the station. We need to make sure no one associated with this weapon gets away."*

"Done," my familiar replied quickly. *"Whatever you do, do not kill this witch. I have a feeling the other entity is already gone so she is our only link to whoever stole the ax."*

I sighed with relief knowing Tseki would have help. *"It will be my pleasure to question this bitch. I have no doubt that there is more at play here but I can't get a sense of what, yet. It's not outright Dark."*

"That's what concerns me. This witch doesn't likely know much, but she will know enough. Something is off. I can't tell because I'm not there but this feels alot like a setup."

I opened my senses and sent feelers out around me. The witch throwing a punch at Stella's face felt the same as Stella. It was as if she'd cloned my friend's power. At least on the surface. The ants were back when I probed her but they weren't as strong.

A scream from the front of the police station made everyone look over to see a cop running toward us with his gun drawn. He didn't say anything as he aimed at me and fired. This was a serious breach of law enforcement protocol. The witch that originally stole the ax had to have them under some form of mind control.

"Get down," I screamed at Stella. Thokrum was no longer standing next to me. I prayed that he was still safe and had the ax.

A second cop joined the first, then a third. Bullets started flying all around us. Stella yanked the witch in front of her and together they dropped to the ground. I needed to erect a bullet proof barrier in front of us.

I crawled between the cars and went into a crouch while I pictured a structure in front of us. I didn't spend much time firming up my intent with the bullets literally flying. I cast the spell and heard the shell casings hitting the pavement.

I jumped to my feet and ran for Stella. I grabbed one of the witch's arms while she got the other. Stella looked at me then inclined her head to out our captive. "Magical restraints?"

Nodding, I imagined an invisible pair of handcuffs being slapped around the witch's wrists that would prohibit her from using her powers. "Use *magia rubernation*," I explained to Stella.

The witch jerked her body and pulled at both of us, her eyes going wide when she heard our plans. With a smile, we cast the enchantment enjoying the way white light flashed in circles around her wrists.

The witch started wailing at the same time I noticed Tsekani and Aidon race around the building. Aidoneus said something to Tseki before he pointed to the three police officers who were in the process of reloading their guns. They stowed their weapons before turning around and going back inside the station.

I jerked the witch toward Tseki. "Can you put her in the back of the vehicle? We need to question her about the witch behind this. Unless you found her and took her out already?"

Tsekani scowled and shook his head from side to side. "She got away the second I caught her scent. She thought she was powerful enough to hide it from me. The fact that she couldn't rattled her."

Aidon wrapped an arm around my shoulders as Tseki took the witch by the back of her shirt. "We need to leave this place before I fry every mundie brain here. Where's the ax?"

Thokrum stepped out from behind a tree and jogged to our side. "It's right here. When the thief took off, she hesitated for a second. I think she was going to try and steal it directly from me. I'm certain the only reason she didn't was that she underestimated who she was up against. You four are a formidable force."

I chuckled as we headed for the rental vehicle. "I love it when I'm underestimated. It makes beating a bitch more satisfying."

A wicked smile spread across Stella's face. "It's so satisfying. No one ever thinks I can do anything. I taught that bitch a thing or two. Speaking of, she might have a concussion. Not that it matters at the moment. We need to pick up some dinner on the way home. I'm famished. We haven't eaten since we left the house earlier this morning."

"Let's order some sushi," I suggested as I climbed into the passenger seat.

Thokrum wrinkled his nose. "I'll take chicken if they have any."

Aidon and Tseki also placed their orders as Aidon pulled out of the police station. My head throbbed and my body was sore in places, but overall, I wasn't in bad shape. I took that as a sign I was getting better at fighting back. I added that as another win for the night.

Just goes to show you that you can do anything you put your mind to. I had a lot to learn still, but I was making progress and that's what mattered.

CHAPTER 19

*S*tella had ordered enough food to feed an army which was good because Tsekani could eat enough for five men. Thokrum was kneeling on his chair as he perused the selection in front of him. "What's this one? Is it fishy tasting?"

Stella snorted as she chewed the bite of a roll with crawfish and a hot sauce. "It all tastes like fish to some degree but that one is a California roll and is probably the safest. I'm telling you that this is the best I've ever had, you should totally try it."

The dwarf picked up a piece with his fingers, sniffed it then popped it into his mouth. His eyes widened and a smile spread over his face as he chewed. "This is good."

I pointed to the shrimp tempura roll. "Try that one. It's delicious and even better when you dip it in the wasabi infused soy sauce."

Thokrum picked it up and dunked it into the small bowl in front of me. I lifted my hand to stop him, but he had already tossed the sushi in his mouth. He opened his mouth and spit the food out before waving his hand in front of his face.

I couldn't help but chuckle as his face turned red. "That was likely hot. I make my dip with more wasabi than soy. Sorry! Don't judge that based on one bite. I really do think you will like it."

The dwarf coughed then picked up his beer and drained half of it before setting it down. "That was awful. My eyes and nose are still burning."

Aidon clapped Thokrum on the shoulder. "You've been indoctrinated into the fold now, brother."

Tsekani lifted a bowl of fried rice, expertly eating it with his chop sticks which was something I could never eat with the things. "The women are right. Perhaps try plain soy sauce with the next one."

The dwarf shook his head from side to side. "I'll stick to the teriyaki chicken, thanks."

I shrugged my shoulders. "More for me to eat."

"You have to try one more. You said you've been looking for the right woman. Well, let me tell you that saying you are brave enough to eat raw fish is sexy," Stella said.

I was busy wondering why Stella talked to Thokrum about finding a woman when the witch in the corner scoffed. The noise made everyone look over at her. She should have kept her mouth shut. I was hungry and enjoying the food and company until I noticed her watching us.

I got up and crouched in front of her. "Are you ready to tell us who you're working for?" I called electricity to my hands and watched as lightning crackled all over my palms.

It was a beginner spell, but most witches could only hold the energy for a few seconds before needing to discharge it. It's why it wasn't a very effective offensive weapon.

She sneered at me. "You might be weak and inexperienced but I'm not. I stole the ax and altered it to do what I needed."

Stella came over and joined me while the guys continued to eat. "Do you have any idea who you are talking to?"

The witch narrowed her hazel eyes. "It doesn't matter. I can get out of your restraints anytime I want. I'm simply biding my time."

That made me throw my head back and laugh. "You're not the only one that's told me that this week."

"Wasn't that the master vampire? And where is Marius now? Oh, that's right, he's dead," Stella interjected.

The witch scooted back and flattened herself against the wall behind her. "You're the Pleiades? How is that possible?"

I narrowed my eyes on the witch. We'd asked her name during the drive home but she'd refused to tell us. Seemed like the time to try again. "You know who I am and I have yet to learn your name. Care to tell me who you are now?"

The witch closed her eyes. "I'm Miriam. This has gotten out of hand."

Stella leveled Miriam with a dark glare. "You think? You attacked us and tried to steal something that didn't belong to you."

Miriam's face lost all color. "Look, I was approached by a woman with a foreign accent about procuring the ax. That's it."

"And I'm Mary Poppins," I muttered.

Miriam glanced between Stella and me. "So, you're not the Pleiades, Phoebe Dieudonne`?"

A sigh escaped me as I waved my hand through the air. "Yes, I am. What kind of accent did this witch have? And what is her name?"

Miriam threw her hands in the air. "I have no idea what her name is. All I can tell you is that she has black hair and dark brown eyes and her accent is a cross between Turkey and Spain."

That ruled out Mile's tart for sure. She didn't have black hair or an accent. I was relieved to put that worry to rest. I didn't have to have any further contact with the awful woman.

Refocusing on the matter at hand, I wondered what did a Spanish-Turkish accent sounded like. *As if that matters right now. You have a murderer to catch.* "Have you seen her around? Do you know where she might live?" I asked, praying for any piece of information that might lead us to her.

Miriam shook her head from side to side. "I have no idea. I'd never seen her before she approached me and told me I would get a power boost without the risk of becoming Tainted if I retrieved something for her."

I pinched the bridge of my nose. "God bless the idiots of the world. No amount of magic on the planet can keep you a Light witch. You've just taken the wrong side in the magical world. That weapon belongs to the dwarf. Taking it and its power is tantamount to stealing it directly from him. That Taints you no matter how you look at it."

Stella stabbed her pointer finger in Miriam's direction. "There are no technicalities that can get you off for murder, either."

"That's right. I suppose she told you killing two innocent people wouldn't get you a one-way ticket to Hell, too," I added.

"Hey now," Aidoneus called out from the table. "Technically it's called the Underworld and the Furies take the evil to Tartarus to be punished for their misdeeds. Of which, murder is at the top of the list."

Miriam wrapped her arms around her knees and was visibly shaking. "I didn't kill anyone. I swear. I don't even know what you're talking about. I just met the witch today. I was going after the ax at the police station. The woman assured me it would be easy to procure."

Tears filled her eyes then fell down her cheeks. I stifled the sympathy that welled up inside me. This witch might not be our murderer but she was willing to steal something that did not belong to her in order to gain more power.

It was witches like her that became Tainted in the first place. Instead of being happy with what they had, they became greedy for more and took it. She never once said anything about being sorry for trying to steal the ax. Nor did she acknowledge the attack on us.

She would become a repeat offender, so to speak and I had no idea what to do with her. If I let her go, I had no doubt that she would up her crime next time. "You should never have been willing to steal anything that doesn't belong to you."

Stella tilted her head to the side. "It's clear she's TSTL. What are you going to do?"

"What's TSTL?" Thokrum asked around a mouthful.

Stella looked over her shoulder with a smile. "Too stupid to live."

I ignored the sob that escaped Miriam and pulled out my phone. Hitting the contact for Mahon, I lifted it to my ear. "You've been a busy girl, Phoebe. Seems like you handled some of the mundies at the police station for us and took the weapon."

I swiveled away from Miriam to hide my wince. "Aidon erased some memories, but not all of them. Your cleaners should still check what they recall of the shifter. I have a witch here that needs to be taken to Coldwater. She attacked us and tried to steal the ax so she could absorb its power."

Mohan's sigh echoed through the tiny speaker. "Is she the one that murdered Ellen and Edraele?"

I shook my head then realized he couldn't see me. "No,

she was approached by a black-haired witch with an accent who asked her to steal the ax from the police station. Can you pick her up and deal with her? Or do I need to ask my familiar how to teleport her there?"

"Can you even do that? You don't know anything about such spells. You might send her into a volcano," Stella blurted.

Tsekani snorted. "At least our problem would be solved."

Mohan chuckled, clearly having heard the conversation. "Let your friends know I will be there shortly. Text me the address and I will contact the warden and let him know to prepare for transport."

That got my attention. "Do you use magic to get prisoners there?"

"Yes. Every paranormal officer has a charm that opens a portal directly to the processing room at the prison," Mohan explained. "It's the safest way for prisoners to be sent away. It ensures they can't escape and perpetrate more crimes. I'll see you shortly."

The line went dead before I said goodbye. After texting Mohan the address, I cast a barrier around Miriam so she was unable to hear our discussion then returned to the table.

"What are you thinking?" Aidon asked as he pushed a plate of food over to me.

My stomach was in knots at the moment and I didn't think I could eat more, but I loved how he took care of me, so I accepted and nibbled on a piece of tempura asparagus. "We need to track this other witch down. Thokrum, can you trace the magic of the rune to the one that altered it? Which reminds me. Can you tell what her changes are meant to do?"

The dwarf lifted the ax from the floor next to his chair. "This one was meant to enhance the user's strength. It has been twisted to a point I don't recognize. These symbols are foreign to me."

Aidoneus picked up the weapon and bounced it on his palm. "It's far heavier than it should be. It has soaked up additional energy which tells me these markings are designed to allow for that."

I leaned closer to him, seeing the crude etching through the elegant runes Thokrum had created. "What are they? Do you recognize them?"

Aidon shook his head. "They look like they could be Sanskrit or Sumerian, although nothing that I recognize."

My heart sped up thinking my mate knew the oldest languages on the planet. I shouldn't be surprised at this point in our relationship, but I was.

"Can you do some research, so Thokrum knows how to deal with them after we find the witch?" I asked.

Aidon smiled at me. "I'll make some calls and see what I can find out."

There was a smile on my face when I turned to the dwarf. "Would you be willing to try and track the witch that stole this and altered it?"

Thokrum scratched his beard for a couple seconds as he stared at me. "It's not going to be easy, and I can't guarantee anything, but I am willing to give it a go."

Tsekani set his chopsticks down and sat back, crossing his arms over his flat stomach. "I've been thinking about that since I broke through the spell that was shielding her. I don't know how I did it, but I know that it's possible. The same magic that hides her scent is concealing her location."

"*Tsekani makes a good point. You should piggyback on Thokrum's spell, Phoebe. Your best chance at detecting the perverted version of Blood magic she is using will be working together.*"

"*I was wondering when you would weigh in, Tarja. I will be sure to let him know. Is there a way to protect us from any blowback she might try to send through the enchantment?*" I knew we would have to open ourselves which would leave us vulnerable.

"I will handle keeping you and the dwarf safe so you can focus on locating her. She isn't going to make that easy for you."

My chest tightened at the thought of Tarja putting herself at risk given her pregnancy. *"Are you sure it's safe for you? I will not risk the babies."*

"Don't worry about them. I have Zeph who can help shield the kits. You need to get rest and recover from today. You're going to need all of your energy."

"I'll have Aidon and Tseki keep an eye out tonight, since the ax is with us. Thank you for having my back, Tarja. You get some rest, too."

"Did Tarja have a suggestion?" Stella asked.

I chuckled and nodded. "Yeah. I'm going to join you when you cast your spell, Thokrum. Between the two of us we should be able to break through her enchantments."

The dwarf sighed as a smile spread across his face. "That's wonderful news. I've heard from relatives in England that a coven of three witches have joined Fae and witch magics to create new spells that are tilting the magical world on its axis. This is exciting."

Fiona had told me about that which is where I'm sure Tarja got the idea. "I'm good friends with Fiona. We're actually coven members."

The more I thought about joining with the dwarf, the more certain I became that we would be successful. It would be vital that I got a good night's sleep so I could face her once we located her. I wanted this over and done.

CHAPTER 20

A smile spread over my face as Aidon's lips traveled across my shoulder. "Morning, Queenie."

I groaned as I rolled over. "I wasn't ready to get up yet."

Aidon's mouth was hot on my neck as he kissed a path down to my chest. "It's almost one in the afternoon. Thokrum's been complaining about having to sit around."

I jolted upright knocking my forehead against Aidoneus's chin in the process. Rubbing my forehead, I jumped out of bed. "Damn, I haven't slept this late since college. You should have woken me earlier."

Where the hell were my clothes? Not that I cared about standing naked in front of Aidon, but I could feel his eyes devouring me and we didn't have time for a distraction no matter how good it would feel.

I spun around then stopped with a chuckle when I saw my bra hanging from Aidon's finger. "Looking for this?"

I prowled over to him and went on my tiptoes then pressed my lips to his. "I don't remember this ending up over there last night, err this morning."

"Then I did my job right." His smirk was sexy as sin, not that I would tell him.

"Are you sure about that? I'm still walking seven hours later," I teased as I put my bra on.

My body was languid and well-rested which was a small miracle after being up most of the night. Showering before collapsing into bed probably helped. Mohan had taken longer than expected to retrieve Miriam. Of course, I had wanted to see how he transported prisoners so I knew first-hand how it worked.

In the end it was extremely uneventful to witness. Mohan had a charm that he used to activate a portal. The most exciting part of the process was watching as the witch was shoved through and to a waiting guard. What we could see of the room reminded me of a clinical laboratory. The walls and floor were white and the fixtures were stainless steel.

Once Miriam was secured at Coldwater Correctional facility, Mohan informed us that they'd managed to catch several of the police officers who were not present at the station the night before. I counted that as a win, even if they still had the databases to deal with.

Apparently, they left the electronic trail for last. The reasoning was that without anyone actively working on the case, the chances were slim that they would come across the files. Whereas it would be a much bigger problem if they were working on the case but could not locate the information or evidence.

I was just grateful we didn't have to handle that part of the case as well as locating the witch responsible. My cell phone pinged with an incoming message as I was pulling on my underwear and pants.

I jerked my chin at the side table. "Can you check that?"

Aidoneus scooped up the device then went stock still. The hair on the back of my neck prickled when I saw his reaction. Rushing to his side, I glanced at the screen in his hand and my blood boiled.

"That jackass just keeps living up to his reputation," I growled as I read the message from my attorney. I hadn't had time to give him a heads-up. Honestly, I didn't think Miles would move that fast.

Aidon handed me the phone and started pacing. "How did he have his lawyer file a lawsuit already?"

My movements were jerky as I pulled a t-shirt over my head. "I have no doubt he asked her to start working on it after the holidays. He blamed me for the kids not visiting him."

"He is incapable of accepting any responsibility for how those around him regard him. That will never change. It's everyone else's fault." Aidon followed me out of the room.

"You must be talking about the ex," Tsekani said as we walked into the kitchen.

One of my eyebrows lifted to my hairline. "You must be psychic."

Stella snorted. "There's only one asshole that blames everyone around him."

I chuckled and inclined my head to Thokrum. "I apologize for sleeping so late. I'll be ready to get started after a quick phone call to my attorney."

The dwarf's gaze bounced between the four of us before settling on me. "I'm happy to wait while an ex gets roasted."

There was a story behind that comment. Thokrum had been burned by an intimate partner at some point in his life. I bet he had some stories he could tell. Hoping I had time to learn more about him, I set the issue aside and pulled up Callum's contact.

"Well, hello, Phoebe. How are you doing this fine summer day?" Callum asked by way of greeting when he answered my call.

Moving to the fridge, I grabbed an energy drink, deciding I needed more of a boost to deal with this bullshit. "I could be better. Please tell me that Miles isn't going to be able to milk me dry." I popped the tab and took a sip of passion-fruit-flavored goodness. I might be able to pay him, but I didn't want him to get a dime from me.

Callum Burke chuckled on the other end of the phone. I'd inherited him along with Hattie's magic, money, and company. He was a mage that she trusted with everything, and I in turn did the same.

"I told you when we met that there was no way your ex would be able to stake a claim on your money. He is tired of paying you alimony and child support and this is his way of trying to turn the tables on you. Little does he know that the way I've structured things your income is cut in half from what it was when you were working for Hattie. This suit will only get him a big fat bill and a bigger alimony payment."

My jaw went slack while my heart leaped in my chest hearing his words. That was the best news he could have ever given me. "Are you serious? He's going to have to pay me more?"

"As soon as I'm done with him, he will wish he had never filed this bogus petition," Callum promised.

A broad smile spread over my face as I faced Aidoneus. "That is precisely what I needed to hear right now. I have a vile witch to locate before she kills again and don't have time for his shit. Before I get back to it, is there anything you need from me?"

"I have everything I need at the moment. I'll be in touch if anything changes. In the meantime, steer clear of him. He's going to be upset when he sees our response," Callum advised.

I thanked him and hung up the phone. Stella pounced the

second I was off the call. "Alright, spill the details. I want to know how that call turned your frown upside down so fast."

I rolled my eyes at my best friend, wanting to tease her for her comment. It was something my mom used to say to me anytime I was sad. I told them what Callum said as I fixed a plate of stir-fried rice that was left over from the night before.

Aidoneus's expression smoothed out and his demeanor relaxed while Stella was full on laughing. Shoving another bite into my mouth, I focused on my familiar. Tarja responded immediately. *"I'm here to ensure nothing happens to either of you."*

"I was thinking of having Stella add her power to the mix. I know she wants to be involved in this process." I still felt bad for making Stella stay in the car last night at the station.

"I would have her save her energy for the confrontation. We have no idea exactly what we are facing, so Stella should reserve her strength. It's possible this attempt will alert the witch, so you guys must move quickly before she can cover her tracks."

"I hadn't thought of that. Thanks, Tarja." This was reason one million and one why I loved my familiar.

Setting my drink on the table, I took a seat and gestured to the others around the kitchen table. "Let's get started. Tarja just pointed out that we will need to be ready to move as soon as Thokrum and I locate her. Before we get started, did you learn anything about the markings, Aidon?"

Aidoneus shook his head from side to side. "I sent Thanos a picture, along with Korros and Viaz. None of them had ever come across it before."

Thokrum set the ax on the wood between us. "Are you ready? We need to channel the element of power infused in these new lines." He pointed to the etchings that looked like Jean-Marc's attempt at letters in pre-school.

I nodded my head and placed my hands on their sides

next to the weapon. The magic tingled against my skin like bubbles in a bath. It was earthy and warm. When I dug deeper, I felt the edge that would slice me in two if I pushed too hard.

"Her magic is sharp," I noted out loud.

Thokrum shifted in his seat, moving closer to me and the ax. "It's like a razor. Hold the element in your mind and focus your intent on it."

Stella cleared her throat. "Are you sure that's her and not just the changes she made to your runes?"

Thokrum scowled at Stella. "Of course, I'm sure. I made the weapon. I know foreign energy when I feel it. This is her residual power. If it were her runes, it would lash out at us when we probed it."

Stella's cheeks turned pink. "I meant no offense. I was curious. I grew up a mundie like Phoebe and don't know all the nuances."

The dwarf patted her shoulder. "You'd hardly know you weren't born a witch."

Stella's smile grew and she nodded her head. I went back to focusing all of my energy on the witch's magic, and my desire to have it lead us to her, while I waited for Thokrum to do his thing.

It took a few seconds before I felt the dwarf's magic flare and reach out. I silently chanted a booster spell and latched into his energy. Dizziness swamped me as his power moved through the earth and spread out over the city. I'd never been connected like this to the planet before. I swear I could even smell fresh dirt as we worked.

It was fascinating to have various small life forms brush up against my awareness. Sweat poured down my back as I funneled energy into Thokrum. I grunted when we came up against a block. It was as if a steel wall came down, cutting us off. The tendrils of his magic felt along the edges but there was no way around, the barrier seemed to go on forever.

I buckled down my focus on burning my way through the shield and pushed that into his energy. Whisps of his power stuck to the blockade and I pushed heat into them. Sharp pain ricocheted throughout my skull making me cry out.

Aidon crouched next to me and growled. I ignored him because the iron pokers disappeared a second later. That had to be Tarja keeping them away from us. When I rejoined Thokrum's main efforts, I noted his tendrils were working their way through and he was tiring.

Pouring more of my energy into the dwarf, I maintained my focus on finding this bitch and not letting anything stand in the way. We remained in place, picking at the site like you would a scab over a wound.

I have no idea how long we worked at the same location until we managed to get through. It was like cracking the thick layer of ice on top of a pond so you could get your fishing pole in the water.

Thokrum's light magic floated through the other side seeking the owner of the dark magic. A gasp left me when I felt his hook sink into the fish we sought. A gasp left me as I jumped to my feet.

To my surprise, Aidon stood there with the car keys in one hand and my shoes and the dagger Sebastian made me in the other. He handed me the weapon and boots then tugged me to the front door.

Thokrum snatched up the ax and followed with Stella and Tseki as we left. The five of us were loaded in the car and on our way before I managed to find my voice. I shoved my feet into my shoes then turned back to my friends. "Be careful. We don't know what this witch is capable of doing. And, you stay back with that weapon, Thokrum. We don't want her to get her hands on it again."

"I will protect it with my life," the dwarf promised before shouting, "turn left."

Thokrum continued to give Aidon directions to the witch. Within fifteen minutes, we were parked down the street from a house in a residential district.

The neighborhood looked like what you could find anywhere in America. And it just so happened to be in my old neighborhood. A band tightened around my chest as I considered the location. It was far too close to Miles and his tart for my comfort. If I hadn't seen the spell at work at the site of the shifter's murder, I would suspect Miles's girlfriend really had killed Edraele.

Their proximity aside, I was nervous about being around so many family homes. If mundies heard a commotion, they would call authorities and come running to see what was happening. I couldn't expend as much energy as it would take to cast a spell protecting the innocents around us.

My gut was in knots and my heart was pounding against my ribcage as we got out of the car and snuck up to the house being sure to steer clear of the streetlights. I held up my hand, halting everyone behind a row of hedges.

I crouched below the top of the bush. "Aidon, you and Stella take the back while Tseki and I approach from the front. I want to try and get an idea of where she is inside the house before we go charging in."

Aidon sent me a smoldering smile from where he was standing behind a tree a couple of feet from me. One corner of my mouth twitched, appreciating that he allowed me to do what was coming natural to me rather than taking over. I had no doubt he had a better way to address this situation, but he wasn't imposing his will on me.

Shaking my head, I looked at Thokrum. "Your job is to stay here and hide the ax. Only get involved as a last resort. If she senses it, she will be on you like white on rice."

The dwarf tightened his grip on the weapon. "I'll make sure she never gets her hands on this again."

Aidon and Stella walked down the line of hedges before they moved onto the property where the spell led us. I followed Tsekani as he approached the front of the house. He moved in close to the building and plastered himself to the siding, then pointed at the picture window.

Nodding, I went into a deep crouch that I would regret later. The muscles in my thighs were quivering as I held my position and lifted my head just enough to see that there were curtains drawn on the window. Moving to the middle, I peered through the small crack in the fabric.

There was no one in the office beyond. At least that's what I assumed the room was, given the large desk in the middle. My heart hammered in my chest and all I could hear were my rapid breaths. Turning back to Tseki, I shook my head then walked in my crouch to the other window on the front of the house.

I was about to check the room when Aidon and Stella came running from the backyard. They stopped at the side of the house closest to me. Aidon bent down with a grim expression. "The witch has Miles inside the great room attached to the kitchen." He'd whispered his words but they landed like bombs in my head.

My breath caught as my hand flew to my mouth. I had no love for my ex but he was the father of my kids. There was no way I could allow anything to happen to him. A curse left me as I opened my senses to check for any wards.

There were none along the property's edge and there were none around the house itself. I doubted this was where she lived full-time, otherwise I'd expect to feel protections all around us. I'd bet this was a location of opportunity. Probing a little deeper, I sensed her magic but it was contained, telling me I was feeling her body.

I gestured to Tsekani then looked back at Aidon and Stella. "We move now. We can't let Miles get hurt."

I would have one chance to cast protections around Miles and I needed to use that to my advantage. Keeping my mind focused on a shield surrounding my ex-husband, I charged for the door. Tsekani beat me to it and kicked the panel off its hinges.

I raced inside the house shouting, *"protego!"* My magic exploded out of me before I ever laid eyes on Miles. The witch hissed and yanked her hand away from Miles's throat as I ran into the room at the back of the house.

She shifted her pale green eyes my way and smiled. "Good of you to join us, even if a little unexpected. I've been eager to meet you ever since you took out Myrna. She was one of my favorites."

My heart stopped for several beats. This black-haired tyrant had to be Zaleria. I hadn't thought about her for many months. Not spending more time trying to find her was going to bite me in the ass. "Tseki, get Miles out of here."

I didn't waste time checking to see if my ex was injured. We were facing a powerful enemy. Right then the witch's hands shot out and a bolt of black lightning shot from her and headed for Tseki and Miles. The dragon shifter was fast and managed to scoop up my ex but the energy slammed into his arm and made him go spinning.

Stella ran into the room, steadying him at the same time I tossed a fire ball at Zaleria. The witch's head spun in my direction and she snarled as my teal flames burned the sleeve of her silk blouse. She spun her hands in a circle and the ground shifted, knocking me off balance.

Stella's pink flames were flying around the room while Zaleria tossed magical missiles amongst the flames. One hit the floor between Aidoneus and me with a loud thud. It dented the wood beneath our feet making me jump to the side. Aidon leaped into the air to jump over the dent before he cried out and fell to the ground, bleeding from an injury to his thigh.

Zaleria's wicked smile grew as she flicked a wrist in my direction and more magical missiles went flying. I'd lost control of my flames and they were now burning their way across the room, so I shut them down. I wanted to end this thing with Zaleria before she got away and that couldn't happen if the house burned down around us.

"You can't beat me, Zaleria. Give up now." I taunted her while tossing magical bombs at her.

One managed to hit her, taking part of her left thigh with it. Blood poured down the outside of her leg as she screamed at me. I turned, helping Aidoneus to his feet as Stella joined us. The three of us faced Zaleria. Aidon was pale and panting while Stella and I had our hands clenched into fists, ready to fight.

"You are far more predictable than I could ever have imagined. Thank you for making this trap one of the easiest I've ever set," Zaleria gloated.

I scowled and took a step, closing the distance between us. "What are you talking about? You're facing a god and a Pleiades. You're in over your head, bitch." I was less than a foot from her now and could smell the acrid scent coming off of her.

Zaleria narrowed her eyes at me as she threw her arms out at her sides and shouted something in a foreign language. Several things happened at once. Stella cried out at the same time Aidoneus did. They were both blown back into the walls behind them while I was thrown into an invisible wall.

Something in my shoulder cracked then I slid to the ground. My head lolled to the side, and I saw the blood pouring from Aidon's. His eyes were closed, his chest barely rising and falling.

I scrabbled to my hands and knees looking at my best friend. Stella was groaning and holding her bleeding side. She reached for me, but Zaleria yanked me up by my hair. "Looks like it's you who are in over your head, Pleaides."

I tried to claw my way free as she held tight to me. It didn't help that I was still stunned. I'd failed this mission. Yes, I discovered who the killer was but she was likely going to kill me.

Not a chance in hell. Shaking myself out of my funk, I renewed my attempt to get free. I managed to swing a leg around and hook her injured one. The second she let go of my hair, I crawled toward Stella.

I never made it because Zaleria recovered faster than I expected, kicking me in the side of the head. The last thought I had before darkness claimed me was to send an alert to my familiar. I didn't want to overexert her given that she was pregnant, but she was my best bet for survival.

Download the next book in the Mystical Midlife in Maine series, Demonic Stones & Creaky Bones HERE! Then turn the page for a preview.

*P*ain brought me out of my rest. My mouth started watering as nausea battled with the agony I felt everywhere. Try as I might, I couldn't stop from hurling my guts up. All I knew, for several seconds, was the heaving of my stomach as food and liquid evacuated my stomach. My eyes watered, blurring my surroundings and making it impossible to see anything.

God, why had I drunk so much last night? I couldn't even recall the evening. I hadn't done that since my college days. I hated feeling like this and made it a point to stop before I got to this point. What the heck had happened to make me forget that experience?

Oh, that's right. Miles had his attorney serve me with a petition for custody of the kids.

I still didn't remember letting that get me down enough to drink myself into oblivion. I tried to lift my hand to wipe my mouth and discovered I was tied to something. I pulled with all my strength but could budge what felt like ropes around my wrists.

I shook my head and immediately regretted it as the

world swam around me. It felt like there was a tiny dwarf inside my skull hammering away at the bone while searching for the sharp, pointy gems hidden throughout my grey matter.

I needed to stop and take stock. I hurt everywhere. It was as if I'd been put through a wood chipper. Alright, that might be extreme because I was still in one piece, but it felt like I had been cut to pieces.

Where was I? Who was keeping me captive?

I sucked in a breath as my memory flooded back to me. Stella, Aidon, Tseki and I had been tracking the murders of an elf and a shifter along with the theft of a magical ax. When we'd discovered the perpetrator, she had my ex-husband captive and we'd gone in magical guns blazing and walked right into her trap.

Zaleria had somehow managed to incapacitate Aidoneus who was a gGod of the Underworld. Granted she'd only been able to do so because we walked into the house where she had her Dark enchantment carefully set.

I can't believe I'd been so stupid that I didn't probe the contained energy further. I'd assumed what I was sensing was the witch herself and didn't want to alert her to our presence. My mind was sluggish as I tried to replay the events, and dissect them, to pick out the magic she'd done. Zaleria had worked more than Dark magic in that house. I had sensed something more, but couldn't put my finger on it.

I shifted and cried out as my back and hips hurt like hot pokers from the infernos of Hell were stuck in strategic points for maximum discomfort. My body was not made to sit on a hard wooden surface. God only knows how long I'd been shackled in the chair.

There was nothing in the room to tell me what time it was or how long I had been there. The chair was a plain wooden one, similar to what I have had around my kitchen table for years. For all I knew, she could have taken it from Miles's house when she kidnapped him.

The thought of him brought my racing mind back to my friends. A vice closed around my heart when I recalled Aidon bleeding profusely. A gasp escaped me, and tears filled my eyes, when the last image I had of Stella followed. Tsekani was injured when he took off with Miles over his shoulder, so I had no idea if he was hurt further when the trap went off.

I knew with certainty that Aidon and Stella were seriously injured. Logically I knew Aidon was difficult to kill and despite the seriousness of his injuries, he would likely recover. That didn't erase the worry eating a hole in my gut.

I could scarcely breathe when I considered Stella. She was my best friend and had become one of the most important parts of my life. She wasn't hard to kill like Aidoneus. Her body was fragile like any other mundie alive. Yes, she was a witch, but I didn't think she inherited a sturdier system along with her magic.

Her injuries weren't as bad as Aidon's. She'll be alright. The reminder fell on deaf ears because the pessimistic side of me that rarely surfaced was busy making up for time being suppressed and pointed out that Zaleria likely killed her, Aidon, and Tsekani before taking me wherever she had me now.

We weren't in the house. My focus returned to my surroundings and I noted the cement floor, metal walls, and high ceiling. Aside from the sour scent of my vomit, the place also smelled stale and moldy, telling me not only was it old, the ventilation was crap as well.

There were no windows in the place. I could be below ground or in an interior office. Regardless, aside from me, the chair was the only thing in the space. I was too weak to break the restraints keeping me in the chair and my magic was smothered under a thick blanket at the moment.

My heart started racing as I scrambled to grab hold of my power. It was still there, but I couldn't reach it. The cloak keeping it away from me was Dark with an undercurrent of malevolence that made me nauseous. Then again, it might be the pain making me sick to my stomach.

"*Tarja?!*" I cried out mentally, hoping my familiar could answer me. The pressure inside my head that followed my plea started the heaving again, only this time nothing came up with the efforts.

I was hunched over in the chair for several seconds until the stomach spasms stopped. My muscles were sore making my back pain intensify. As if that wasn't bad enough, the pressure in my skull kept shooting through the roof every few seconds.

It had to be Tarja trying to reach out to me. I couldn't take much more. "*Tarja, if you can hear me, stop trying to respond. It's making the intracranial pressure in my skull skyrocket. I have no idea what's going on. Zaleria kidnapped me. Aidon and Stella were hurt badly, send them help. I pray they aren't dead. I can't access my magic. I'll never stop trying to find a way out of here.*"

The pressure stopped, making me sigh in relief. It was good to know that whatever was keeping Tarja from responding to me, it didn't stop her from hearing me. Unfortunately, that relief was short lived. The pressure continued to ebb and flow like a river.

I needed to get away from the mess I made on the floor. Pushing my feet against the ground, I scooted the chair back a couple of feet. It wasn't enough but that had taken most of the little energy I had at the moment. Perhaps I could hop away.

Focusing on pushing my feet down into the cement while lifting my butt, I managed to bounce up and back another few feet. Sweat broke out across my forehead as I continued to hop my way away from the throw up. I made it about ten feet before exhaustion made me stop.

I wanted to pull my minky blanket over my head and go to sleep. With the amount of pain that I was in, I doubted I would be able to sleep, but it would have been nice to try. Obviously, that wasn't an option. Hell, I'd give anything to lay down on the hard cement ground at that moment. I desperately needed to change positions. The discomfort in my hips, back, and ass were growing to the point they were over taking the pressure in my head.

I have no idea how much time passed before the door creaked open behind me. I hopped and forced the chair to turn. I was expecting Zaleria and was surprised to see a young woman with short dark brown hair holding her nose as she stood in the door.

I noticed the shimmer of runes carved into the doorway as she pushed off and crossed the room to me. "I've been told to move you to a room where you will be more comfortable. Damn you stunk this room up."

No matter how hard I tried, I couldn't use my magic to get out of my predicament. It had to be the marks in the door. Thankfully, I was far more accustomed to reading people's body language without magical input.

Working from the assumption this woman was evil, I watched as she waved her hand in front of her face. Her grimace was replaced by a self-satisfied smile before she approached me. No doubt she cast some kind of spell over her mouth and nose to block the smell. That meant the room wasn't warded to ban all magic use.

Lifting my chin, I looked up at her. "Where are you taking me?"

One hand went behind her back. When it returned to her side, she was holding a small knife. "Don't try anything stupid. All you'll do is cause more suffering. You won't be able to get out of here, anyway. It's impossible unless you know where the exits are located."

She sliced through the rope of one wrist and for a second, I was tempted to try and take the knife from her. Her warning flashed through my mind, stopping me. I was weak and my magic was suppressed. I needed to bide my time and get the lay of the land.

When my second wrist was free, I jumped to my feet, almost falling over in my haste. The woman stepped away from me and held the weapon out in front of her, leaving me to stumble into the wall a few feet away.

Once I had balanced myself, I twisted my torso trying to work a kink out of my back. "My name is Phoebe. If we're going to be spending time together, it would be nice to learn your name."

The witch narrowed her hazel eyes and jerked her chin in the direction of the door. "Not that it will do you any good, but my name is Eirina." She pronounced her name eye-reena. That was an odd name, not something you heard often.

I took a closer look at the witch and noted the sharp cheekbones and slight cleft in her chin. Thanks to the pain and dizziness, I didn't need to try and hide my smile. My cheeks wouldn't move.

Au contraire, Eirina, this information will help me more than you know. She inadvertently gave me leverage I might be able to use over Zaleria. That's assuming the Dark witch cared about her daughter. Before I tried to play that card, I would have to observe and gather more information.

If Zaleria cared about her daughter, I would be able to use Eirina against her. But the chances of that were probably slim to none. Zaleria had proven to be nothing more than a power-hungry witch.

A chill hit me when we walked into a wide hall. I shivered

and wrapped my arms around my chest as I scanned my surroundings, while also trying to get a feel for my magic. Wherever we were there was little to no heating. That furthered my theory that we were inside an abandoned warehouse. However, all these rooms didn't fit what I knew of most facilities like that.

Passing through the doorway hadn't affected me like I thought it might. I blamed whatever was smothering my magic. The concrete theme continued as we passed three closed doors. Try as I might, I couldn't connect with my magic, nor could I hear anything behind the panels that might clue me in to our location.

There were at least three more rooms ahead of us, all with their doors were closed. At the end of the hall, an aisle branched off to the right. Eirina paused at the fourth door along the hall. When she moved ahead of me to open things up and let me in, I looked back to see what was behind us. Aside from the open room where I'd been held, there was nothing. The space dead ended.

Eirina pulled me inside the room when I continued looking for a way out. I grunted and yanked my arm from her grasp. "It's good to know you weren't lying. This luxury is unexpected. Why is Zaleria keeping me here?" There was a bed and a bucket inside this small room.

The obvious reason was so she could obtain my powers, except they had to be given freely. She couldn't steal them from me. And I would never willingly give that vile creature one ounce of my magic.

Eirina rolled her eyes. "This room is a dump. Barely a step up from the holding cell."

Normally, I would have said she was right. Having endured enough time strapped to that chair, I nearly wept at the site of the mattress. Every cell in my body was crying out for me to lie down and take a load off. Which is exactly why Zaleria had kept me in that room for so long.

I needed to see more of the building. Turning around, I crossed my legs as if I needed to use the bathroom. "Can you take me to the restroom before you lock me inside this place? I'm sure you don't want to clean up another mess."

Eirina laughed at that. "I won't be cleaning up anything. That's your bathroom, right there."

I grimaced when she pointed to the bucket on the corner. "Do I at least get toilet paper?"

"You'll be lucky to get food and water. But know this, I don't make the decisions here, so do me a favor and stop asking." With that Eirina shut the door in my face.

I limped to the bed and sank onto the mattress. It might be marginally softer than the concrete slab beneath my feet but it felt like a cloud. I bent to remove my shoes then thought better of it. My feet didn't need to breathe that bad. It was better if I was ready to act on a moment's notice.

The fresh smell that greeted me as I laid flat on my back was a bonus to having the bed in the first place. It was good to know Zaleria cared enough to do laundry. If only she would bring some water. I was dying of thirst after throwing up everything I'd consumed the day before. That was going to hasten my dehydration.

As if my thoughts conjured her, the door opened and in walked Zaleria. My body shot upright faster than I thought possible. My legs refused to hold me when I stood up and I fell back to the bed.

Zaleria lifted a bottle of water. "I thought you'd be thirsty."

I scowled at her and wanted to deny the offer. Instead, I snagged the bottle and twisted the cap. It hadn't been opened before, so I sucked back half of the bottle before I knew it.

I was hyperaware of Zaleria as she walked into the room

and stood in the middle with the door open as she spun in a slow circle. Screwing the cap back on the bottle, I set it on the floor next to the bed. "Why did you kidnap me?"

Zaleria's light green eyes landed on me. The look she gave me chilled me to the bone. "For your power of course."

I scoffed, or tried to. The sound that escaped me was part snort, part groan as my head swam. My vision swam for a second. I needed to get out of there. The water had been nice, but I was seriously injured and sore all over. "I will never give it to you."

Zaleria closed the distance between us and crouched in front of me. "Is that right? Myrna told me it would be impossible to capture you because you mated a gGod of the Underworld and yet here you are in the prison that I designed just for you. And it was pathetically easy. You don't even like your ex-husband and yet you rushed in to save him from me. Breaking you will be just as easy, mark my words."

I shook my head and toppled onto the bed. There was no way I was facing her lying down. Mustering all the strength I had, I lifted one leg and kicked Zaleria in the chest. She fell back, landing on her butt.

She rebounded before I did and managed to punch the side of my face as I was pushing my body off the bed. We collided against one another. I grabbed a fistful of her black hair and pulled. Zaleria lifted a hand and shot a burst of black magic at me.

It punched the breath from my lungs and I staggered away from her. It felt like she'd cut me but the oily magic I'd felt dripped off of me. I have no idea why because I couldn't use my magic. That damn blanket was still smothering it. Not to mention I was unsteady as hell and was hanging on by my fingernails. My body wanted to collapse while my eyes slipped closed.

Zaleria's expression darkened when she saw me still

standing. She tossed one spell at me after another in rapid succession, all concentrated on my chest. My shoulders jerked each time they hit and it became increasingly harder to get any oxygen.

I was happy to say that oily crap stayed out of me. It felt like an important win. It would be short lived if I didn't do something. My Nina would never be able to stand up to a witch like this. I could not let her win this fight by killing me.

Then Zaleria shifted from magic to her feet when my body finally gave out and collapsed to the ground. The good thing at that point was that I didn't feel half of her blows. My body was beyond that point.

I tried to reach out to Tarja one more time, but stopped when the pressure fluctuations made me worse. I crawled to the bed and pulled myself onto the mattress while Zaleria watched. I didn't have the mental capacity to predict what she would do next.

I couldn't be sure if she had drugged the water or if she'd cast a spell on me. All I knew was the world continued spinning around me and I could barely keep my eyes open. Zaleria said something before she left the room that I didn't hear. I was too busy trying to calm my racing heart and find a comfortable position for my battered body.

Giving up on finding the right position, I closed my eyes. My grey matter alternated between feeling like it was being compressed and feeling like I was floating. You would think that would be enough to stop my racing thoughts, but you'd be wrong. They continued running wild before they settled on one thought to replay over and over again.

Your friends are dead, you're never going to see your family again. You will fight Zaleria until the bitter end when Nina will become the Pleiades before her time.

AFTERWORD

Reviews are like hugs. Sometimes awkward. Always welcome! It would mean the world to me if you can take five minutes and let others know how much you enjoyed my work.

Don't forget to visit my website: www.brendatrim.com and sign up for my newsletter, which is jam-packed with exciting news and monthly giveaways. Also, be sure to visit and like my Facebook page https://www.facebook.com/AuthorBrendaTrim to see my daily posts.

Never allow waiting to become a habit. Live your dreams and take risks. Life is happening now.

DREAM BIG!

XOXO,

Brenda

ALSO BY BRENDA TRIM

Hellmouths & Hot Flashes

Holidays with Hades

Bramble's Edge Academy:

Unearthing the Fae King

Masking the Fae King

Revealing the Fae King

Midnight Doms:

Her Vampire Bad Boy

Her Vampire Suspect

All Souls Night

Made in the USA
Monee, IL
06 July 2022

99194346R00132